Trauma Is My Business

ER Journal

Mitch Bensel

Trauma is my business.. ER Journal

This is written in fractured sentences with dots that cause a flow of pause:: for this is a journal :: enter as the saying goes, at your own risk:: Graphic:: Based on real events...

Thank you God for helping me through life.

Trauma is my business ER Journal

Based on real events. **A fictional journal,** any resemblance to any persons, place or things living or dead is purely coincidental..

For my mom ::I hope you enjoyed all the souls
that said

hello to you from me, after they died

For my dad... love you poppa

Mom and Dad... till we meet again :::

rest in that place of love...

:::: slip reality into the sands..

fall gently against yourself

::fly ..

My father passed away as I finished writing this book. He didn't recover from an open heart valve surgery....He was 88 years old and the greatest man I have ever known, or will ever meet. I walked into the room just before he passed. The nurse turned to me and said, "He must have waited for you, because his heart just stopped." His hand was warm. I touched his still warm forehead.

I have seen so many this way but not my dad. Strangely enough I didn't cry ..yet.. I asked him to tell mom hello. His finger tips began to turn blue. I have seen this also, but not my dad. They will put him in a body bag and slide him onto a cold slab in the morgue to wait for the funeral types to pick him up. I have done this very thing, to hundreds of bodies. Before I reached the hospital, I felt a liquid kind of peace move through me. I know..it was my dad.... now both of my parents are in that place of love, where we all come from.

Driving home I did cry.. I yelled with screams of profound pain..I would always start my day of work, wondering who will die today. When I walked through the door of my home, the sun was just coming up... today was the day, my father would die .. love you poppa…

Trauma Is My business

ER Journal

Mitch Bensel

Prologue

Forty four, I loved that age. I was freshly divorced after a twenty two year marriage of not happy, with abuse on the side. Verbal abuse can shoot a soul into the corner of 'oh hell', with a flick of tone and a wiggle of the abusers toes.

After a divorce and closing of my martial arts schools, I turned to the medical world to find a grown up job. My martial arts my love, my passion was considered a waste of time. For over thirty years I taught this art to thousands. Helped many with their self esteem and gave them the tools to handle many life situations. I on the other hand fell away from the path of cool and strength into the weakness of soul and flesh.

I started with EMS working at first with a slow, transport only ambulance service. Taking sick people to and from doctor's appointments was not my cup of medical tea. But after just a few weeks with that group the more advanced type EMS hired me. Yes there I was working where all EMTs wanted to be when they grew up, all the action, every possible injury. But after lifting one too many I left that job to the young ones of good back.

Now I work at a level one trauma hospital in the heart of the land where people go when they get hurt, an emergency room. Mix that with the fact it's the general hospital of the state so we get every type of human being. I think for my sanity I need to write the dailies at the ER. I am an emergency room tech. I can bag your freshly deadness, draw your blood, do compressions on your chest, EKG you around the block and the one duty of non fun, give you a bath. In other words, I am your body mechanic. You come to my ER a tad broken; I help in sending you home shiny clean and given one of our famous sandwiches.

I am given a chance to be with people that are at their worst and scared to death and of death. Of course some have a lot of anger and some, well for no better word, are insane. But hey aren't we all just a bit?

First Thoughts

Walking toward the beach I look down at my feet while they move across the pavement. My black boots, beaten a little from old EMS days, seem to be my only friend. One that has seen everything I have, been through the blood as I have never judging me just sturdy under me. As I think of what will be in my day of work as a tech in the emergency room. I know there will be the usual of fresh dead with tears and screams from the ones left behind.

Breathing deeply I pull in the ocean's air. Memories and moments collect them use them to find perspective to pull away from reality when that parking place becomes too strange.

:::::::

……. I watch as they drop his right leg onto the floor. Blood spurts interestingly when you open an artery. "Nice rhythm," I say, as his legs are thrown to the floor, torn from his body by a motorcycle sliding down the highway…. A sense of one of those 'strange' moment's hits as I find myself pausing any thoughts of sorrow or pain, just the ocean, or the trees leaves, the way they do love the air to move them. Call me crazy, call me calm, call me an idiot, but one has to find a way to handle, reality, that reality being life and working in an emergency room of a level one trauma hospital.

My desire to be in the middle of the emergent in need is getting old, “like me, I’m old.” My voice is small near this magnificence.

The ocean seems to be able to remove my visuals temporarily, of death and the family members screaming at the dead body to wake up. I still hear her voice, scared and worried calling me to get her grandma more blankets because, “her skin is just too cold, wake up Grandma, someone needs to get her a blanket she is too cold.” I mix these memories now with the ocean. As if the ocean’s current becomes the artery of my very existence. With each waves push, the ebb of tide fills with images, voices, feelings, tears, pain. I hear the mother of her 25 year old. The daughter did cocaine the daughter’s heart stopped. I am the lucky recipient of the mothers anguish, the ebb of tide allows the visuals to fly.

"Oh my baby please don’t let her be dead,” screams with sobs are an interesting combination. They subside then gain pitch with the next exhale. Yes, the beach releases for a moment the voices and the memories of the mix of death and the clash of life. But not for long.

Finally reaching the stairs down to the sand and ocean I feel a familiar presence. A jagged kind of spiritual presence, the same feel at times after someone dies. Someone that is not of good energy and a little upset they are dead. I throw this thought aside quickly. Not wanting it to know I am aware that it is near me. Ghosts, spirits, energies, whatever you want to call them, they tend to find me. And I am not in the mood to have them invade my haven, my ocean.

The prison guard my watch, announces the need to go to work. Waving to the universe of sand and water I bow bidding a farewell. The ocean is a woman, has to be a woman. The way it can so easily captivate, engulf and roll you up onto the sand aching and hot waiting for her moisture once more to satisfy your reach.

Head down as I walk, enjoying watching my boots move across the sand I come across a treasure. In the middle of the dark round stones that cover parts of this coast is an agate. It is translucent and full of magic everything has energy and rocks have the coolest magic alive. Sometimes just feeling a rock in my pocket, can still the fear in my heart. Fear or sadness they both fall into the same boat.

Climbing the stairs I remember one of those spiritual gifts I used when I was young. With just a glance, or thought, I can look at you and into you. Your soul doesn't hide from me. Perfect none of us are, and I can see the shadows that reside within. What use is this gift? I have no idea. Maybe I am to observe and learn the ways of energy life and death. Maybe it is for protection so that I can shift the reach of negative bad energy away from me.

My father once wanted me to dream the outcome of a horse race. He still enjoyed a good game of cards or a night at the casino. I just had to mention that I wanted to see the winner before I went to sleep and voila, it would occur. But no dreams today, just the ocean and reality of my choice to work in an emergency room. Back to work. My Astro van waiting for me, on this day it looks like a guard, watching over me waiting to carry me to work.

--------The portal

The parking lot is full so that means I might be a little late. This hospital cares not if you are a minute late or if you are sick or even involved in a car accident and show up in the ER. You will be given a disciplinary action and two points. Common sense is a dead beast. The point system has thrown many away from the doors of this hospital. Mayville is a teaching hospital where everyone wants to work. So people are like fodder easy come easy go.

As I pull into the parking lot of the hospital, I see one of the nurses getting out of her car. Most are attractive, this one is very attractive and out of my reach. I am just a tech I continue to watch the nurse walk towards the hospital. I am doomed to always see the hidden sensuality of women. It is in everything they do.

My stride quickens, to catch up with the nurse. A hint of her scent filters through me. She must be aware I am trying to catch up to her, because she turns, smiles, but continues walking without pausing or slowing. “It’s hard to be a tech.” My voice small once more but not because of an ocean’s surf, because of my own lack of self esteem.

The staff door to the ER is next to where the ambulances park to bring in their wounded, faking wounded and sometimes, already dead people. The ambulance bays are already full. The day will be long the day will be hard. But, the day will have nurses to look at. I toss my badge up to the box that will magically unlock the door.

……

Cool factor...........

There are factors in my life; cool factor is an important one. May not have much but damn I’m cool. The cool factor in teaching martial arts for thirty years left me when boredom found my roundhouse kick. I closed my schools and stopped the cool factor of martial arts.

The cool factor of working in a level one trauma emergency room is fading now. I have the burned out phase hitting my every moment. . One does get tired of death. Especially when the most beautiful of life is outside waiting for me to come and play... play consists of cycling, or working on the agates and shells I find to make jewelry. Wrap it with a leather strap to wear around the neck and you have the cool factor.

My day by choice is one of screams, blood, death and stench. The familiar rot of flesh or toss of blood dried against the skin. Being spit on, swung at, and yelled at, from angry sick people.

Ah my wonderful moments of wiping feces off the wall and off the patient's hands, after they literally pulled it from their own bottom while standing on the stretcher, "just tired." Again my voice finds the air. Even my talking to myself has increased and if the saying fits the answer, I am crazy in the lands of normal folk. Normal folk, why am I always trying to find the niche for me? The normal folk should step my way, life is beautiful. Lean your head, toss a smile at the flowers, the sun, the air that reaches, and reaches for us to feel it. Most do not, some inhale it others wish it would cease. Normal folk are boring.

Walking through the doors of the ER I clock in quickly. Glancing to the bloodied patients that lie in their ER bays, while heading to the locker room, I imagine pulling as much light around me as possible. That spiritual stuff that most people don't even know exist covers me like a layer of vaseline when I need it. Those energies of dark and nasty will just slip off around me.

Immediately upon walking into the emergency room I see the eyes of red and swollen from a young lady, as the chaplain walks with her toward the made up viewing area, for the fresh of dead. It is one of the ER bays, but with the surgical light put on low and angled against the wall. The light of low tries to give the feel of a comfy place.

I watch her body begin to weaken as I walk past her. She is getting closer to the closed curtains. Behind door number three is her husband or child or friend, cold with expression, and always with a tube sticking out of their mouth. Cannot remove anything until the coroner says it's ok. As I turn the corner, I hear her screams begin with that sobbing rhythmic crying.

Now is the time for that wish to know what to do or say to someone. How can one say, "don't worry we are all going to die? or, '"they are gone little one but will always be with you." That makes no sense to someone that is looking at their dead person they knew, and loved for their whole life. If they are gone then why are they still here, why can I touch them? So the answer to the sob is allowing it to happen.

When my grandmother died the air changed around me with a vacuum of silence that took years and years to leave. I do not like death. Even with the understanding of forever being where all will go, I do not like death. It’s like an echo without an echo that echoes. The mind can move quickly into thoughts of past even when you don't want to think about the past. Just bam and a memory of something painful hits. The lineage of a bad memory thought, I see someone die, I hear the loved ones scream, the mind decides I want to access death memories and there it is. In a flash of a few seconds my mind can fly to the very day I suffered the pain or loss or whatever fits the category.

My dog Skitch, was really the family dog, but I always claimed him as mine. Skitch, named after the conductor of Mayvilles Orchestra, was a French terrier of fast and happy that didn’t belong in a cage when we left the house. So just before the door was locked, and my family of six was in the car, I ran over and let him out of the cage. Yay! But no yay. When we returned home Skitch had torn up several rolls of toilet paper and gleefully ran through the house, literally covering just about every inch of living space with toilet paper.

My father took out the belt, and the lean over so the leather strap can hit my bottom, began. Gritting my teeth, refusing to cry, because if one did cry when getting a spanking, with belt or hand, who knows what would happen.

The words “don’t cry or I will give you something to cry about,’”just had an ominous ring to it. So the tears never occurred, just a grit of teeth and searing pain. As punishment to the dog, Skitch, was put out in the backyard. But someone decided to cut through the yard and left the gate open allowing Skitch to run away.

Frantically running through the dark night, calling his name, I looked on the ground near the street and there was Skitch. Blood pooling around his mouth and his body smashed. The thought of a pancake slapped me in my wee mind. The air shifted then inside me, and as I ran back to my house, I sat outside alone and cried like a baby. It was my fault my dog died “my fault,” I whispered into my tear soaked hands. The practice of push and shove emotions away began then. And it never left.

Watching my boots walk down what has turned into a very long hall, my mind returns to the moment of now in the ER. My mind zooms away from the memory of Skitch lying in blood and the feel of that smack of silence and death. In the middle of the pull are flashes of all of the people I have seen smashed blown open, ripped apart by concrete or bullets. The locker room door is a pleasant pause, softening and removing the images.

Removing my P-coat, I lift the trauma shears from my locker. My mind falls back to the rhythm of the ocean. Walls inside my mind slam down to protect. Tears wiped away. Tossing that aside, I smile to create the false of happy and try to find the fun in every moment.

“I am healthy,” pausing as a hint of back pain filters across, “not wealthy," visions of the past when money was not a worry, marriage and a house of large now gone with divorce. Finishing my thought whispering, “and maybe wise.”.....

Slip into my thoughts

For life flows like water

The waters for my toes to rhyme

The waters of flow and mine..

Cool is this place with colors of

flowers of sun and shine......

Night shift is done and wants away. It is time to give report to the oncoming tech and nurse, the passing of the torch. I listen to what I have in store for me for the start of the next twelve hours. A chorus of vomiting, with curse words flying from behind one of the curtained rooms, tells me in a new york minute what is in store for me. A scream from the back of the ER causes all to turn to see what the noise is about. Just... another dead moment and the family member not liking it at all.

I have a lot of chest pain people today, which means redundant blood draws and EKG's with the occasional real MI occurring, MI, myocardial infarction, aka, heart attack. I have to admit I do love phlebotomy. I do it well and don't hurt the patient, too much. Getting the appropriate supplies to draw blood I turn to begin a day of long.

“Are you Ms. Lights?” “Yes,” she says dryly. Leaning I check the arm band to see if it matches the blood label. Have to check and make sure so I don’t get the wrong blood, or the right blood but the wrong person. The butterfly needle is a handy quick way to get blood. It’s called the ‘butterfly’ needle because it has little flaps to the side and when opened it looks like a butterfly. The flaps are to grasp as you shove the needle into the patient’s vein, or gently slide, depending on the vein and the mood of the blood taker.

Veins can be interesting animals and become more interesting when one draws blood for a living. With a gasp and an ‘ooo nice veins,’ followed by a reach to touch the pulse of said protruding vein, is a common occurrence with blood takers. Surely if vampires live they must do the same, check out the veins on that neck!

In the hospital most people are sick and dehydrated or drug users or very old. All of the above offers not the best veins to get blood. When the needle goes in, the vein says no thanks and collapses. Skin can also be rough from using them at work or rough from time but there are some people with very, very tough skin. The skin is so tough that when the needle is pushed into the arm it literally bends. What does one tell a patient when their skin bends a needle? Are you an alien? is my famous retort to the skin of iron.

Some veins are huge creating a sense of over confidence. 'Oh you have great veins I will get you easily with one stick.' Ok something about huge thick fat veins, is they have huge thick fat walls, and something about the over confident phrase of, 'this will be easy', causes the gods of phlebotomy to cringe.

The needle goes in and no blood return, nothing, nada. Embarrassment 101 is when the tech has to go ask the phlebotomist to please get blood from that guy in bay three, that has huge tree trunk veins, but I can't get a drop.

There are veins of juicy and wonderful, but as soon as the needle goes in and the excitement is found. It blows. It leaks around the puncture spot, and begins to fill like a balloon. Skin pushing ever upward, causing the patient's eyes to get very wide, followed with a, "what have you done to me!"

The needle is near the skin, the patient is calm with head turned not wanting to see a metal needle inserted into their flesh. Right as the needle begins to pierce their skin, they scream and yank their arm away. Well, the moment that all phlebotomist's fear has just occurred. The needle is hot, meaning there is blood on it and can infect you. The needle is also in the air falling. How fast can an old martial artist move? Fast. Evading once more a sharp from finding me I grab the patients arm and yell 'Don't move!' Before the patient can recover I push a new needle in to capture the much needed, always wanted, blood.

He had tattoos of death and skulls with grim reaper flying across skin, muscular and taught. When I walked in to get his blood with the little butterfly needle, he began to cry like a baby. 'It's just a small needle dude calm down.' I said this to him as I sat to ready him for the stick. But his tears don't slow, pushing the needle in I look once more at the tattoos wondering why he wears such macho, if inside there is such weakness. People do like to hide their true self. For in life does anyone know who they really are?

Back to the way of blood, I look at the next patient I have to stick. She is a young woman of distress, life has not been kind to Ms Lights, as lines of worry show on her face. She could be considered beautiful, but the edges of her choices are showing, those choices of alcohol, smoking and drugs.

So death is what she wishes for but some how this time it didn't happen. Her wrists are covered with bandages but dried blood is on her forearm. The standard of cutting the wrist must have come to visit her mind. The ones that truly want to die usually succeed. Ah, the ones that have tried, make up a large percentage of visitors to the emergency room, at least to this one.

There was the man that continued to overdose on various drugs from Tylenol to alcohol, finally finding success in the wish to cease to exist by falling in front of a fast moving train. That is not very good for the health. The ER receives his broken body. Legs on the side in two coolers, completed this picture of suicide with success. Although we did chuckle at the fact that he had the lower half of his body over the tracks. Yes cold and heartless we chuckled, perspective and disassociation are blessings to medical workers.

A self inflicted gunshot to the chest. A sixty year old man, it seems, had enough of this land. But he wasn't going to get it done this way. He thought because he carried a DNR , do not resuscitate order, that if he hurt himself a little, the hospital would let him die. NOT, it's against the law to try to kill oneself, so his rights are gone and lost and we the hospital must do all in power to make him live. It could have been an attempted murder etc::: have to follow the dots of laws in the lands.

Another took enough Tylenol to kill his liver. Nothing we can do but tell them they will have a very painful death. Eyes do widen when the reality of accomplishing something that was meant only as a way for attention. Now the death is near and its front porch is not the comfy look they expected.

A lady on the phone with her son, distressed and lonely tells him she wants to kill herself. The son laughs at her and yells at her to do it or he will come over and do it for her. She rolls into our trauma room with half of her head blown off. "She did it, she is already dead", he tells the story as if bragging. Not one family member visits, to view her body. Dwayne, one of the nurses jokes as he points to some of the brain matter now lying on the edge of the sheet next to the hole in her head. "Look kindergarten." I smile at this attempt of humor, as I shift my thoughts quickly away from her life of play, and school, and children. As I put her in the body bag, she watches me with dead eyes. Just like all of the deads eyes, glassed like, fake. Factoid number one on fresh dead types, their eyelids never seem to want to stay closed.

I have spent many a moment trying to push them closed, lift them, hopefully then get caught by the lower lids lash only to have the eyelid slowly open while I zip up the bag.

They seem to want to peek at me. So of course I speak to them, telling them to find peace and tell my mother hello. One lady of death's left eye just kept opening slowly, just her left eyelid. She is my winking lady. Zipping the body bag up closer to her face I continued to push gently to press the lid against the lower lash and hope it would hold. But as I zipped the bag, the eyelid would slowly open once more. 'Peek a boo,' words that come out of ones mouth in places of just not normal, are usually ones of humor. Like icing on a cake, have to smooth the horror and reality of death.

He was retired, his head was opened by a bullet that entered correctly into the bottom of his jaw, exiting through the top of his head. The exit wound always larger allowed for his brains and blood to find easy escape.. I looked at the wound closely, and the angle, and positioning, he definitely knew where to place the gun. For a moment that flash occurs, and I see the life of this person, a wedding, a wife, children, and a time when voices of pain kick once too often causing a choice of no return. The gun placed perfectly.

Like a turn of the channel, I see another one of GSW to the head. The hospital vernacular for gun shot wound. He was with his family, walked outside to the front yard. With one pull, he bought a special trauma bay suite bay number four, with the appropriate surgical light placement once more against the wall.

Falling back to the moment of now, in the reality of blood, I resume my normal blood drawing duties and look down at the patient, another one wants to die.

"So, where shall I get blood from you today?" People know their bodies better than anyone. They definitely know where the best veins are located for getting blood. Watching as she slowly leans to her side a little, exposing an arm covered in bruises. Pointing slowly and groggily she says, "Right there is the only place you can get my blood. And I will give you only one shot then you are done." How many times have I heard that statement, sometimes with a threat of death and dismemberment, if I don't get their blood with one stick, people don't like to become pin cushions.

"Piece of cake little one, one stick fills many tubes." Applying the tourniquet I see the wonderful swell of vein call to me. Pushing the needle in easily, filling the tubes of blood needed for the different tests, removing the tourniquet and poof. 'Did you get it?' "Already in, and finished, and out." She opens her eyes and lays her head back on the stretcher. “That’s the only good thing that has happened today.”

Walking back with the blood tubes to the lab desk I hold my head for a moment. Handing the blood to the phlebotomist, “will you send this to the lab for me?” She takes the blood with a quick, “Sure,” hesitating she sees something is not right in my Denmark. ‘What’s wrong?’ Lenny is one of the cool ‘phleebs’a nickname used for phlebotomist

“Just not feeling right today Lenny.” Lenny is one of the comfy souls. Finally getting comfortable in the one of phlebotomy, she helps many of the patients, because she is good, she doesn’t hurt them. Another of my fav phleebs is Kathy. She feeds us wonderfulness by bringing in yummy things. We call her Granny and she is one of comfy soul like Lenny.

The sudden hallowed, horrible sound of a head slamming into the floor is heard. There is no other sound in the world as someone’s skull crashing to the ground. Making my way over to the now thrashing patient lying on the floor, ‘we have a seizure!’ His head bleeding from the smash against the floor, causes the visitor with the patient to scream. That’s what the loved ones do.

Slipping a towel under his head to keep him from hurting himself more as the seizure continues. Turning the patient quickly to his side, to try to allow a good airway, I wonder what it would be like to have a seizure, causing your body to jerk tightening every muscle as the mind leaves reality, slamming your physical to the floor or against the wall, no control at all. This man has the intense seizures with every muscle tightening. A good work out in my mind, some seizures are just light rhythmic movements while others are like this one full out muscle tightening moments. The only problem with this work out is that the muscles can only do it for so long. After a time the kidneys begin to fail due to the 'sludge' from your muscles that clog the way to filter. The name for the breakdown is a cool one, RHABDO.

The trauma buzzer makes its horrible buzz sound calling me once more to the back of the ER to the Trauma room. Vera, one of the techs and another favorite of mine, comes over to take over holding the patient on their side and keeping the towel under his head. So I can have the pleasure of working the trauma room.

Walking quickly into the trauma room I see a lady with blonde hair that is covered in blood. An interesting way to become a red head, as thoughts of re-arrange occur once more, now in the world of reality any red head I see, a flash of blood dripping through, will visit my thoughts in one quick flash.

I remove the patient's clothes, tag her with temporary identification, and get her temperature. Getting a temperature is interesting, either by mouth or by bottom, it will get done in the trauma room. Her blood is beginning to cover the backboard, her screams are of that agonizing kind, intermittently, she asks questions, repetitive questions. I have learned that repetitive questions usually mean only one thing, a head bleed. The brain has some bleeding, and the patient goes into a repetition mode.

Because of her head trauma and repetitive speak, I cannot get an oral temperature. A rectal temperature is in order. I can usually get them quickly, depending on the patient. Some tighten their legs to the point of almost breaking my wrist as I position the probe to find its resting place. Unable to use the normal thermometers, we are made to use the disposables. Well those are very short. So usually getting a rectal temperature means getting very up close and personal with the patient. The penis is in the way a lot of times. Having to lift it to then slide my finger slightly inside the rectum to mark the spot, now insertion and voila! On this lady and this day I get it quickly. Passing the vagina, my finger finds the opening of the anus and slight insertion, followed by the probe. She fights me for a moment, calling me John then speaking out of her head, "John don't touch me down there I told you only Jimmie can touch me there."

The room just continues with their duties, but smile as one of the docs tells me, 'Yea John stop it'. This trauma room is used to seeing and hearing everything, so a simple mention of who has the use of her private areas is nothing out of the ordinary, everyone continues to help her. The meds are ordered and X-ray people come in ready to shoot whatever is needed and quickly. Quick is the word of the day, pushing the new docs to think fast on their feet. The patient is still screaming on the stretcher, a Jane Doe, no identity as of yet.

Her face now seen clearly as the doc wipes the blood with a towel, then begins to staple the lacerated scalp together. Her skin falls away from the bone that protects her precious brain matter. Interesting the way the skin falls away from our bones, the skull sometimes in tact, sometimes cracked, with the ebb and flow of the arterial bleed, almost hypnotizing the watcher. We are fascinated with the body's interior, showing it to us while we 'practice' medicine.

Her brains are inside that protective place where they belong. Her skull is intact. Here goes a click and a trigger, as eight thousand more moments to fly to my mind. My thoughts find the times when brain matter was on the sheet next to a freshly opened skull due to a bullet. Or the nice touch of a hatchet, slammed perfectly into the skull. A butcher knife has an interesting slant, when it is left inside the skull..

Or the backboard splattered with brain matter. In a moment the mind does show when triggered, every opened skull that my eyes have ever seen. Then the images shift to every head that didn't quite hang right off of the body. Hanging oneself puts a twist in the get-a-long. The head off to the side, with a stair step look as the spine angles outwardly, wanting so badly to escape the hold of skin.

Back to reality my mind releases me for a moment to the now, with the staples clicking into place, soon her head will have the Frankenstein look with shiny metal.

The docs are busy, working on her fractured leg to put a temporary cast on, they call it 'reducing it'. It stays on sometimes for longer than a few minutes.

One more time::::::::

Ah, my trauma room, always the trauma tech never a trauma ....be? It is trashed from the last body that rolled through. Gloves thrown on the floor, blood on the floor, anything the docs and nurses use is on the floor. Even with garbage cans wonderfully supplied in easy access places, everything is always thrown to the floor. I will call for environmental services to help me put the room back to await yet another sad soul that has driven under the influence, or hit by a car while walking or just medically unsound and the heart ceases its rhythm.

I enjoy people, observing them, teaching them, watching how they interact. One doesn't have to have the monies in the world to be a cool person. And I like to watch the all of people. One of my favorites is Thelma, a wonderful African American lady of time and age, works harder than anyone in the environmental services department. "Hey Thelma Lou," smiling as she walks in, Thelma begins her speak of the things bothering her I wish I could give her enough money for her to retire, she deserves it. Works hard, has worked hard her whole life, never got much of an education and is now working on her GED at the young age of fifty two. "Jared you are wearing me out," she sweeps up some of the tossed ortho glass used to splint the ladies leg. The blood on the floor is about to be gone. Thelma is thorough. She never complains of the work, she takes hardly any breaks and she always makes sure the rooms are clean.

Time for the song of the day, "For once in my life I have someone who needs me…." Thelma smiles at me as I stop in mid lyric. Tossing a blood soaked kerlix into the red garbage bag of bio waste we laugh. The trauma room is a wonderful place to sing, all avoid it at all costs, and release of the reality of our mortality is in the way of song. As Thelma walks across the room I see she is limping. "Thelma what's wrong? You are limping?"

She tells me of her back or her leg or something is not right and she hurts. So I think for a moment to try to find a way to touch her lower back without looking like I am trying to assault her.

Hoping to see, wanting to know, if maybe I can help her with my gift to heal. Sometimes the push comes to me, or the nudge to just reach and touch someone. The rest is up to the big guy, whether or not they are to be helped by my touch that pulls for light to find their pain.

Will it stir the lands of the universe and all the good little angel things that walk this place? They do exist, yea, believe it or not. Energies of light and dark walk around waiting for us to call on them to do our duties of help or hurt. Some people though deserve a little smack in the souls face. That is also up to the big guy. The big guy is God to me or whoever you want to call, or say is the creator. At least in my book of psalms that is who the big guy is. People don't understand or believe much of the spiritual lands. They especially don't understand those that can lay hands on to heal.

"Show me where it hurts."

Moving my hand behind her, I touch where she is pointing to the spot of pain. Lightly now I am able to hold my hand near her lower back. But now, how can I continue holding my hand here without her thinking it's strange. I have to keep my hand near her back for a bit, to feel if there is an exchange and to pull light, well never mind on the details, I have to find a way to keep my hand there. 'Jared what are you doing back there it feels hot?' She asks me quietly, but doesn't pull away.

I just continue to visualize her spine, her discs, her nerves, and mixing with that is my energy, with a thought of strengthening anything that is weak or healing anything that is broken. My hand is hot and I pull it away from her back

"Thelma I don't know what's wrong back there darlin, but I can try to fix you if you let me do this once in awhile."

Knowing that doesn't sound right, especially that it is said right when Michele, one of the ER nurses walks in. "Do what Jared?" Smiling she winks at me. "What are you two up to in here?" Thelma grabs her dust mop and just shakes her head. "Jared you are truly wearing me out." Michele gets meds out of the trauma pyxsis. "I'm just messin with ya buddy ole pal ole friend," Michele says as she walks out of the trauma room.

Thelma continues to mop. Turning I look at the blood on the floor then my right hand. It is still warm from my attempt to help

Thelma. But,I am not sure if I can heal, sometimes it works, sometimes it doesn't. With a shrug I finish stocking the bay in the trauma room.

The double doors to the trauma room open rushing quickly in is EMS with another patient. Compressions are occurring so it's obviously some kind of heart failure. Either traumatic or medical, either way the person they are bringing into the trauma room is dead. A traumatic full arrest has a better chance of coming back to life; a medical usually means the heart is just done. A traumatic one is caused by an impact of some sort. Either the patient slammed into the steering wheel or the seatbelt. Sometimes they are thrown from the car and tossed like dolls across pavement which can cause a 'traumatic' full arrest. Thelma moves a little faster to clean the other bay and get out of the trauma room.

Waving them towards me I direct them to my freshly cleaned bay one, rolling my shoulders to loosen them some as I get ready to take over doing compressions. Compressions are a work out with attitude. I am about to get very tired pushing on the chest of a dead person. The patient is an older lady in the normal position of delivery from EMS. That normal position of delivery is one is lying flat on a board with a c-collar with orange straps holding them tightly to the board. Her clothes are of a good quality.

Her head is bleeding profusely down the backboard to the floor of the room. "Start compressions we have no rhythm." Jumping to get the CPR stand I begin the push workout of CPR. The usual occurrence is a rush of docs and nurses pushing many drugs to stimulate the heart into life, while I become the heart by pressing hard on the middle breast bone on the chest, the sternum, pushing against the heart causing it to continue to 'beat' to move the drugs through the body. I am this person's heart beat for the few seconds or minutes of compressions.

But for some reason the doctors don't work too long on this one. They put in one central line to push more meds that try to awaken the heart. But on this lady they call the time of death quickly. Glancing to the side of her head, I see why. There is brain matter all over the back of the stretcher.

They throw off their gloves, to the floor next to the garbage can and walk out of the room leaving me and one nurse in the now still trauma bay.

Imagine the silence, my muscles are tired and flexed, my heart is pounding in my chest but just below me is a fresh dead. No movement, stillness with attitude follows my workout with attitude. The fresh 'dead' is an elegant looking lady. Hair is that silver shine of age and wisdom. Touching her hand I make my wish, that one I do with all fresh deads to tell my mother hello and for them to find peace. A chuckle escapes me as the thought of all of the fresh dead types showing up at my mothers place on the other side of reality saying, Jared says hello.

The story of this one's death begins with a vehicle. Most start their last day of life, in a vehicle or a vehicle is involved in one way or another. She was T-boned. The great expression of being hit on the side of your car, by another car usually traveling at a very high speed. It is a hard hit and one that a lot of people don't survive.

As I lift her head to place a towel under it to soak up the blood so it won't pool in the body bag. My fingers did a horrible thing; they accidentally slip into her brains. The feel of the squish is emblazoned in my soul. Pulling my fingers quickly out of this place where fingers never should go, a whisper escapes with a gush of an exhale 'excuse me ma'am'.

Disrespect to the dead is something I will never show and this felt disrespectful. Now, put with the thought of a T-bone steak, the word or the thought of it will immediately pull me to her brain matter and the feel of it's softness as my fingers slipped into her skull.

Slamming walls down inside my brain, I try not to feel, or see the life of this lady. But a flash happens and does its dance thing through my mind. Her children, her love, her life, is one second of a blip across and the sadness finds me once more. Not really over her death but all death. It's just not natural. I don't like death. The Big Guy should have put post it notes somewhere or something, so we can communicate with our loves of fresh dead. Although, I have felt my mother at times, when the wuss factor hit me causing tears to escape. Tears are a waste of time in my book. Nothing to be done, the sadness is caused by something, but there is nothing...to be...done. I hate death and I hate tears.

::::::::::::::
::::::::::::::::::::.........

The air is hot

water ..cool .jumping high through the

sprinkler, I fly becoming the water. .....soft yet strong...

reaching to find the magic of it's

release from the metal sprinkler

I am lost inside its hold..

The air is hot....

============

The body is moved to one of the bays in the trauma room, to allow family to look at their loved one for the first time as a dead loved one. There are patterns in an ER, some days its, knees, other days its strokes, this may be the day to die.

I walked in rain ...of drops so small ...

they filtered easily into my soul...

feet were wet but no matter as yet ..

.for the day only holds so much of this gold

::::::::::::

I was training some new techs once and I could not resist the temptation to startle them. We had a fresh dead, intubated. Sometimes the stuff in the gut comes out of the tube that helps the patient breathe, especially if it's a 'goose' intubation. Which means someone pushed a tad too far down into the stomach of the patient. This fresh dead had fluids moving up and down the tube. Not coming all of the way out, but it wouldn't take much to make that happen. Just a wee little push on the fresh deads belly and the job would be done. I asked to be forgiven as I approached the fresh dead. The newbies were looking at the face of the dead guy. I gently pushed on the stomach. This causes the fluids to push out of the tube in his mouth. They jump back for a moment. Yea, no disrespect and I think the fresh dead dude appreciated the joke?

:::::

Another fresh dead could not stop making burping noises as we rolled him into the body bag. One of the new techs and I were having trouble with this one. The odor hit my nostrils and I think I was going to vomit. Takes a lot to do that....so yea it was she thought so too, was slightly ill. We hurried to bag this dead.

::

Working the trauma room can be an avalanche of death and blood with legs on the side, the floor being the side. The sometimes nonstop thrust of bodies into the small room tests all involved.

After one of the deaths, the doctor of specialty meds pushed on the mans belly, poking it with a laugh, "breathe for me," he yelled then laughed once more. The man not breathing slowly turning that ashen color of the non. He leaned to poke once more into this mans stomach. "C'mon breathe for me!" Said the doctor with his uncaring smile. I watched and waited for him to leave this man alone. I watched, and wished he would not misuse his order in the way of things. I waited to clean the fresh body and place it into a bag. Wishing it a way to find peace. I watched as the doctor walked out with his grin, laughing once more before he poked his finger again.

Where is the compassion, where is the feeling of soul.

The lady lay there on the trauma stretcher, she had already been examined with a broken hip and a broken leg, she was deaf and dumb, yet her screams were still audible. The special ones of areas of concern, the doctors of trauma finally show in the room. Just as we are about to move her to CT scan. "Let's examine her," he said. One nurse spoke softly, "we have already turned her". He looks at her with disgust and says, "How do I know? We are wasting time with this argument." The lady screams once more, as the same thing is done, so that he can bill her for the honor of his touch.

How can life be without such humanity, where did the feeling of touch go, in a place where it is so necessary? Humans, just as we, lying there helpless, waiting to be saved, hoping to be saved. Not wanting to be hurt.

Another patient rolls into the room with more compressions being done. One of the medical students, whose rotation is in the ER this day, helps with CPR while I watch. The patient's stocking is ripped down the side. The stocking she put on to ready herself for work. Now, she lies dead on my stretcher. Her shoe is off to the side, as is her foot. Open fractures of the ankle show the stub of bone for all to see, and the fragile nature of our flesh. Her skirt now carries dark red blood that is coming from her abdomen. I get caught up in the flow of compressions and watch as her leg moves with the rhythm of each push.

Imagine now the morning begins, her lift out of bed is slow, because she is tired. I visualize what I feel was her morning, applying her make up, sitting to slip her foot into her shoe, the one I see now off to the side. Pulling her skirt up adjusting it just right, now the slip into death. Her body rocks with each compression her arms off the side of the stretcher and laying limp with that white cloudy way the skin gets after death. Her feet also have that 'dead' look. The docs said once of a man brought into the trauma room, "he is dead you can tell by his feet." The feet, the skin, the exhale, contain a new learned rhythm.

Sunrise, the start of a beautiful moment, a vision of light falling across green fields onto our back porch, then finding its way to our coffee pot, sunrise, the start of a day that someone will die. I walk to the other bay to finish stocking it, hearing as they call her time of death. Numbers on a clock mark a moment of yet another one of us that slows into no breathing no breath no rhythm of anything. Just dead.

A body bag is needed, and the push begins to rearrange the furniture of my real of reality. I lean to pull one of the body bags out of the supply shelf, waiting for the images and the wonderful flash of the dead ones I have bagged in my years. Kind of like watching an old movie, one of those movies you didn't want to watch because it was so poorly done, yet your mind wouldn't let you turn away. The reach for the bag and voila, the film dumps into the cavities of glassed eyes or bloodied faces. Heads blown open wide with metal of bullets, swoosh, slam, flip. The nudge of lift and the toss away of thoughts occur, as I push with subtlety, death away from my mind

I tie on the proverbial toe tag, usually picking the right big toe. Not sure why, but it is the toe of my choice. The last roll, the body into the swimming pool smell of plastic, my job is done..

The body goes in quickly, lifting with skill, the technique of moving the dead. The bag zipped the wish left in the air for the dead one to find peace and to tell my mother 'hello'.

She will be moved to the morgue quickly away from all to see. But I still see her stockings, and a shoe that just doesn't quite fit well on the foot, dangling with blood following, from a lady that is now dead. Yes what will the sunrise bring.

****

flight of light ...

I whisper to see....

it is always bright and there for me

when sun says hello to my day..

flowers were the path of happy

and time knew no rest as I

played...

the air warm ..my breath

warm..my day

warm..from flight

of light.....from the sun

always watching my way..

saying hello..

****

My redundant walk again as I finish stocking the trauma room. kerlix here, tubing there, syringes for drugs, fluids for the veins. All ready for the docs to find, and the nurses to use. Thelma has already left. Looking around, the room is ready to rock for the next contestant to "come on down." A voice over the paging system once more shrills "Trauma!"

The doors seem to open in slow motion. There are many walking fast with this next trauma. The stretcher moves to its parking spot. The patient is pregnant, full term with a cesarean delivery scheduled the next day. One more day and the twins would have been delivered healthy and alive. The OB docs are called down to the room, baby warmers are moved into place. The skills of all involved are at their highest now. I hear the report from EMS. A car hit her car, she pulled her younger one out of the car, she collapsed. At the time of collapse, we assume that's when the babies were ripped from their supply of oxygen.

Slow motion with speed... contrasts of noise with silence. Blood splatters to the floor as they cut her abdomen open to remove the babies. Baby girl A baby girl B. The docs are covered in blood; they step and walk and move through it, but do not stop their work. Compressions have begun, the mother's heart has ceased. I move to help with compressions.

When the day starts in the ER, it doesn't stop until the clock decides to slow into my oblivion of hell. The ER has been hell, and I seem to be the wheels.

Now I begin my journey. My hands placed on her sternum, she is young in her twenty's. As I do compressions I glance to the left and watch the lifeless little ones fall away from their mother. I push.......I turn away, I look at the face of the mother, I push........ I look at my hands, I push. My only job now is to move blood and medicines through her body by becoming her heart. One of the nurses steps up to me and takes over compressions, as I begin to tire. We put ten units of blood in this mother of twins, we had sixteen more on the way.

I stood for a moment unable to move, watching the skills of the docs, the techs, the nurses. All working with one purpose and one need, and one hope, to keep all alive. Baby Girl A, time of death is called, Baby girl B, little compressions with two fingers pushing lightly, stop their movement....time of death is called. Looking back at the mother, she has a heart rhythm again, we brought her back for a bit. The docs have sewed the mother back together. ...   Gone to the OR they move quickly away. My bay is trashed with blood covering every inch of the floor in that bay. .....They were bundled and put in the same warmer. Baby Girl A, Baby Girl B...I wish you to find peace..and tell my mother ......hello.

It takes four environmental workers to get the bay clean.:::::::

:::::::::

Hanging upside down

I laugh at this world of funny and

sunny, wow life is cool

and crooked..

hanging upside down..

from the branches   of a tree

:::

My trauma doors open and here they are. She is frail and bent and smells of rot. Something has died on this woman and it is her own skin. Her family called for EMS but obviously that is all they have ever done for her. She looks like a person from a concentration camp in the days of the Holocaust. The skin on her back is black and red and very dead. The odor is not one of this life. She lays there with eyes of such a deep sorrow and pain. EMS found her on a floor with straw under her, as she lay in her own feces and urine.

Now she is dying, her heart is slowing its beat. Compressions are called and I instantly grimace at the thought of pushing on this frail soul. Lightly, I begin my push to her sternum. But with this push at times you can have a break of the ribs. A very not fun moment when pushing, and hearing, and feeling, the broken bones move with each push. They began to put in the central lines that will carry meds to her body quickly, and hopefully bring her heart back to the normal of alive. I got angrier with each push on this literal skeleton, at the lack of compassion, and the atrocity of this total abuse, the fear, the pain of hunger, the pain of lack of love. Other med students came in to 'practice' putting in central lines. This is a teaching hospital after all, the lady will be used as a teaching instrument. So I just kept pushing, until the medical students, and the residents were done with their learning time.

Time of death is called. She is free from here finally.. this time I don't mind ..   death.

:::::::::::::::::::::::::::::::

White feathers of soft to find...

that wish you hid in time..

    just whisper my small one of life

and surrounded you will be...

....surrounded   you will be

with love

::::::::::::::::::::

I have an unusual problem when I get very, very, angry I spit.. It just happens, yea that's how it is. Pushing a different stretcher back to the trauma room, I look back at the family standing outside the trauma room, waiting to view their emaciated mother. I want to spit.

The trauma room still smells of her rotted skin. Pushing the new stretcher to its parking place in bay one of the trauma room, I look at the contrast. The room is clean as if nothing has ever happened of blood, or maggots or pain or death.

The trauma doors burst open ripping me from thought. The stretcher has two occupants. One is a patient, the other is the triage tech Angie. She is riding on the stretcher while doing compressions. Whenever Angie is in triage something straight out of TV occurs. His friends drove him to the hospital, they came to the window, and there was Angie. 'Help my friend isn't breathing!' A stretcher is taken to the car. Angie feels for a pulse, nothing. Security literally throws him on the stretcher, while Angie rips his shirt open allowing buttons to fly. She begins to push on his chest as they roll her into the trauma room.

Angie continues compressions while one of the docs tries to get him intubated. An intubation involves some interesting instruments.

A lighted handle and a long silver looking blade that slides into the mouth lifting the tongue so the doc or medic can visualize the vocal chords, and slip a tube through and into the patient, just past the vocal chords, so a machine can breathe for the unconscious patient. Well, this doc must have been flustered. Angie continues compressions, but begins to look a little weak. She is hypoglycemic. I ask her if she wants me to take over but she just waves me off, with a strong reply of, "no I have it." The doc begins to push the blade into the dead mans mouth and lean the head back. But instead of lifting the tongue, he breaks both the front teeth. "Oops," is heard. But this guy is dead so it's ok.

Angie is stubborn, so I run out to the candy machine. Getting a candy bar and quickly return. Opening it, I stand across from the patient in front of her. The docs are putting in their central lines, nurses are putting in IV's and I am pushing a candy bar into Angie's mouth. "Chew!" Angie eats the candy bar without skipping a beat of CPR. Yea just like TV.

Another body bag for another dead. The front teeth broken and bent back, would have hurt a lot if the dude was alive. Something to be thankful for? this day is not giving me much rest. The body moved to the morgue, after the obligatory viewing from those left behind.

Next.......::

The yell begins "Trauma!" I tilt my head to try to make out what this next patient's problem is, as they roll her into the trauma room. I see blood, literally covering every inch of this person. Bright red, slippery blood. As I put the trauma tag on one of her ankles, I notice a french fry between her legs. Her jeans, and shirt and shoes are covered with that wonderful slippery, sticky blood that our bodies spill. They are not even doing CPR, she is dead.

EMS at times will not want to do the paper work required when they have a dead, so they bring them to the hospital. I know of this golden rule, I followed it at one time. No one dies on my truck. So they bring them to our trauma room to dump the paper work on us. A flash of ketchup with fries hits me as I take her temperature rectally.

Yes, one has to be dead but warm and dead in the winter. If the body is cool, steps have to be taken to bring them back. This sad lady is dead, her blood is all over her, the story of her end was an argument with a boyfriend. She drove away fast, eating fries. I will never look at fries again the same way.

The body bag fresh of that shower curtain smell, hides the hideous blood loss. I feel a sadness with this one, she had kids, she had some presents fresh out of lay away for them. They came to see her while I was stocking the bay to the trauma room she just left. “Wake her up grandma, she is so cold.” I close my mind to the thoughts, and the feel of their sorrow but it finds me anyway.

Yes, a dead body, but we are upset about paper work, that my friends, is the way of life in the desensitized zone. After viewing, pushing, rolling, bagging, lifting, cleaning dead bodies, one becomes very used to those dead eyes. They become a laborious project of tagging, and bagging, and paper work. I didn't kill this woman, I don't know this woman, I will wish her to find peace and tell my mother hello as I zip the bag over her head. I zip it over all of the heads that are finished with this place we call life. Paper work and bag work, nothing more or less.

Ketchup will never look the same. "Maybe I can have a T-bone with fries that will complete the loss of my sanity." The nurse in the room doesn't even miss a push of her pen, she is busy with the dead paper work.

Removing jewelry from a fresh dead is a vision of contrast. Taking from them what they cannot take with them. Rings slip easily from blood soaked fingers. Pulling harder than if they were alive I try to remove a most stubborn ring, it doesn't want to leave her.

Hearing a crack of her finger, I realize I pulled too hard. The ring slowly comes off and with it comes the feel of jagged energy, her soul is confused or shattered or something because I feel it now all around me. If you have ever felt jittery on too much caffeine and the air is not comfy, that is what it feels like. 'Go to the light or something but leave here' I plop the rings in the bio bag to lock into the safe. Wanting this energy or ghost or whatever it is to leave.

The story of this one, she had a fight with her boy friend. She got in her car. She is dead.

Quickly wrapping her in a white cotton sheet to help soak the blood. I roll her into the body bag. As I zip the body bag, I imagine her morning, putting on the jeans that are now soaked in her blood. Silence finally comes to the trauma room and this young one. She must have found the light or something because I feel the energy leave.

:::: A Morgue Moment

The morgue is another ...can be... terribly scary, sad place. Security has to open the locked morgue door for me, but they don’t help with the body transfer. It seems that once one of the security guards dropped a dead, so they aren’t allowed to help. Even after death a body is a liability.

The morgue has its own stretchers. They are stainless steel and very cold. I transfer the white body bag and position it in the cooler. I quickly get out of Dodge, because this place is full of spirit types that are confused or angry and stuck here for some reason. I want no part of their after existence.

I have discovered if you show them you are aware of their existence they turn into real pests. Maybe it's like that movie where the lady could hear the dead guy and he found out she could hear him, so he hung around her.

One fresh dead didn't want to be put into the cooler. Something was pushing the stretcher back as I tried to push it forward. It took two security guards and me pushing with all we had but it would not budge. I stopped and said to the dead, "you have to go in there so go to the light or something." With one final push the stretcher slammed into the cooler and we left fast.

Once the morgue showed what must have been a grumpy spirit trapped and not happy in the cooler. I was putting a fresh body in the cooler, and the stretchers were turned over, and some of the body bags were tossed around. This messed with my head, and I was alone on this trip. As I turned to leave, the cooler door began to close. This door has no inside handle, so you are stuck until somebody comes to collect a dead.

Capacity for speed is interesting when the fear of being trapped in a small, very cold room with old dead things in bags becomes a possible reality. Just before the door clamped itself shut, I slammed into it and ran out. I left the ER stretcher down there. it scares me....or as a friend of mine said once "it scares us." I like it so yea, it scares us:::

Walking away from the morgue quickly, I noticed the offices that are parked right near the dead-people cooler. How could anyone work in a room right next to bodies and body parts freshly cut out of someone during an autopsy? I laughed a little, because I know the reverse is thought of with my job by the autopsy people. I handle everything that could ever happen to a person while they are alive, they handle everything after death:: The elevator was slow as usual, not allowing me to get away from the morgue area fast enough.

:::::::::::::Whispers are cool with a slice of cotton...

to feel between your toes...:::::::::::::::::

Back in my trauma room, I do a quick once-over for the stock check. Techs are necessary but not appreciated. The trauma doors open suddenly startling me. Thelma is standing there with her cleaning cart, smiling. "What are you doing standing there like that, Jared?" She pushes her cleaning cart in. "You wear me out," she says as she begins to mop up the blood left from Ms. French Fry. I ask her quickly, "See any EMS heading this way?"

"No, we are done with traumas today." A hopeful thought, but I know differently.

Just as she finishes cleaning the blood off of the floor another trauma comes in. A young girl packaged and wrapped from another hospital. She has a perforated colon.

"How did this happen?" The doc asks EMS for report and all in the room are ready to hear what happened. X-ray is there, ready to do the quick look inside, as are the resident's two nurses and registration.

A whole lot of nurses, docs, and techs are present when a patient is brought into the trauma room. The patient was supposedly having some kind of very rough sex with someone of love. He sodomized her. But with what, is the question. She is torn way up into her colon. I heard the EMS workers mention a pipe. The hush begins in the room when everyone realizes she must have been brutally raped. Moving her quickly to the OR, this young girl is safe now, but will she return to the same abuse, most likely; most do.

Memories find me of all the abused women that have been to the ER. One woman was raped by her husband, beaten, and sent off to the hospital with a story of falling down the stairs. While in the ER, she was visited by her abuser. He closed the curtains and beat her while she lay in the bed. Casually slipping into the hospital bed with her, he raped her once more. A quick few thrusts, and he has completed his terrorism in her world. Now she will feel she can never escape him, for even in the hospital she isn't safe. Yes, abusers know their job, and they do it well. Guess what if she doesn't want to press charges he walks free to do whatever he wishes.

The trauma room is not stilled. EMS rolls in with a lady bandaged around the lower half of her body. Blood is seeping through the bandages. She doesn't stay long in my trauma room. We are only going to get her vitals then move her quickly to the OR also. She has just had a baby, it seems someone was not happy with this and decided to put a gun up into her vagina and pull the trigger. Luckily for her, it was at an angle that shot through her bottom. If he had aimed it straight up into her she would most likely be dead.

A first time of fetal homicide. The husband hit his wife with his fist then pushed his knee deeply into her abdomen. She arrived at the hospital, and the baby was dead inside her. No sound, no heartbeat. What does it feel like to know your child is dead inside you? Fetal homicide is an interesting term. That line of what is life and what is not has been argued in courts for years. I am not an abortion advocate, but that is my path of beliefs. Everyone has choices...::

This reminds me of the partial-birth abortion years, where the parent can decide up to the ninth month they don't want to have the baby. The birth is partial in that the head is exposed. The skull is crushed, and the brains are sucked from the skull. Now we have a baby that can only be killed while in the mother's womb legally if the mother wants not to give birth. If this child happens to slip out and cry or breathe before the brains are sucked out, it's considered murder, not abortion. But if someone pushes his fist into the mother's belly and knees her and throws her against a wall and it kills the baby, it's murder. I am so confused. If this is "normal," maybe I don't want to be normal.

::::::::---

Even whispers know the seasons, to fly and find the walk,

with a breath of fresh color.

gone with the naked of fall, we are alive stripped

for the new..

of this beauty that is our self

the one in the mirror ….

You …

:::::

---Uma

As the trauma room stills for a moment my job becomes one to float in the main ER and help with whatever is needed. The ER is a usual mess, with people scattered about moaning, vomiting and cursing. I look out across my wonderful emergency room at the disarray. A naked older gentleman is walking past every bay, looking into each one, then walking to the next. I walk up to him with a hospital gown in hand, the ones that never quite cover any part of the patient. It's a simple way to tease them with the feel of almost decency, but their parts still hang out the back of the gown.

The old man is talking of someone that most likely has been gone many years or doesn't even exist. This man has Alzheimer's, that nasty thing older types get, that removes proper thought processes and memory. Reducing an adult to that of a child, lost in their minds, in another world, they have to be controlled,, medicated, and watched. I walk him back to his room, "you have to stay on this stretcher ok?" The old man just smiles and begins to stand again to walk past me. I gently pull him back to the stretcher, "you have to stay here, or I have to tie you to the bed." He sits down for a moment, settles into the stretcher but for a moment. In rushes Uma one of the techs, a German lady of interesting ineptness but I do so enjoy her.

"You must stay in zee bed Mr. Johnson." She pushes him back into the stretcher. I watch as she moves around him. He will be restrained soon, but for now Uma has him under control. She is slight of build, blondish red hair and has an uncanny ability to almost kill every patient she comes in contact with. Chuckling at this sight, I like her and enjoy her, she is not very skilled but she means well in her attempts to give patient comfort.

George, an interesting man and tech, walks over to help with the older patient that is a tad out of his head. George has not had much medical experience as of yet, but is working through the classes necessary for medical school. George and I have had many conversations of depth and of shallow of people and of life. George is one of the real people and I have a great respect for him and thankful for the humor that he gives to me to my day. He is the father of three little ones, but his marriage is one of casual.

His parents did not have the best relationship, and he has decided to float through this marriage as is. He doesn't have a belief or realization of love. At least that is what I assumed from some of our conversations. Marriage is just something two people do, to create and raise children and allow time to fall away. George is one who is cool in my mind. He just flows like my poetry, against the winds of normal but into the palms of life. If you don't understand what I just said, then you are normal. "I'm just sayin."

Before George had his children and was still young in his marriage, he came to my emergency room with a wish for a new adventure. He goes through life actually experiencing differing skills to see what he may possibly enjoy. He doesn't look at it like what makes the most money; it's what stirs his mind that makes him search.

This old man will have to be restrained to his stretcher or he will be all over the ER and possibly fall and get hurt. George walks in to make sure he doesn't leave. He is carrying a posey vest, an interesting contraption that looks like a vest but wraps around the back of a stretcher restraining the patient in a safe way. It is not used much anymore but back in the day was quite the contraption.

George is also waiting for a brief to put on this patient. Well, in the way of not much medical experience comes a moment of working through a situation with the best intentions in mind. I have to help another patient onto a bed pan while George begins to put a brief on the Alzheimer patient.

The laughter is silent, walking past the bay to check on the old man and see how George is handling the posey vest. The family is following me into the room.. The curtains thrown open reveals a sight I have never seen the likes of. Uma is laughing hard, but with no sound escaping. Her whole body is shaking in laughter. George is standing near the patient with a look of pitiful. The family questions, “What are you doing to him?” Closing the curtain behind me I tell them quickly. “We are taking care of him, give us a moment.”

The posey that should be tied behind the stretcher, is tied neatly instead around his knees in a very nice bow. The posey vest is on his bottom. George looks at me with the most pitiful look I have ever seen, “please tell me this is a diaper?” Uma runs out of the room laughing all the way down the back hall. “No, it’s a posey vest.” Laughing, I give in to this moment of humor. Removing the posey vest from the old mans bottom while the patient just smiles at me. No harm no foul this dude is in the lands of Alzheimer’s.

“Well I was waiting for a brief and a posey vest, I didn’t know what either of them looked like, I was hoping this was the brief!” George laughed along with me. “No dude, but we will fix it.” Adjusting the old man, making all normal looking once more the family is allowed in. George wins the award for the day for being ….creative.

:::::::::::::::::::

I was walking past one of the bays in the emergency room and overheard the patient's reason for visiting my glorious ER. She lives in a nursing home and told them that something was crawling around her groin area. They didn't listen. This something crawling was eating away her skin, they, being maggots, do that for a living. She asked once more for the people to help her, they did not. She wanted them to call EMS to take her to a hospital. They would not call. If it weren't for a family member visiting her at the nursing home, she would have been lying still in her bed, having her skin being enjoyed by maggots that have made themselves a home.

Maggots are good things actually, maybe a kind of gross feel, but they clean and eat only dead skin. But to feel them eating and crawling on your skin between your legs and have no one do anything, that is beyond a horrible moment. The nursing home has been reported and the family is suing. But the little gentle lady is terrified about going back to a place of neglect.

A man is lying on the stretcher covered in maggots. They are in his eyes, his nose moving with their slippery way all over his skin. Is this maggot day? He was found down in an alley covered with maggots. He smells of alcohol and looks like something out of a zombie movie. The eye docs have to be called in to pull them from the eyes. With a warm wash cloth I begin my techly duty and wipe away the maggots. This isn't working for they are now falling to the floor, and near his shoes, and too near my feet. Wheeling him into the decon room, I lower the shower nozzle to wash him on the stretcher. The maggots fall away into the drain. Interesting job I have. "Thank you for doing this, I'm sorry I'm like this." The man says as he looks down at the things crawling and falling away from his groin.

"Is my job dude no worries." Finishing the task of maggot duty the patient is put back into his room. Fresh gown and sheets waiting for the eye docs to pull them from his eyes, he falls back away into dream land. I wash my hands with the alcohol jell. It slides quickly across and up onto my arms. "No maggots allowed" I turn to the doors of the ER, EMS is bringing in a patient that has a familiar ailment, little white rice things crawling to the top of the patients pants. "Great, it is maggot day."

"Jared?" The charge nurse looks at me smiling, "Please?" EMS puts the patient into a room. I walk him to the decon room. He is a frail young homeless man, hair is thinned black, with specks of dirt and pieces of grass mixing with the premature grey. Sitting the frail one on a chair in the Decon room, I pull down the shower head that will once more wipe away maggots to the drain.

Maggots are crawling under his balls and into and out of his bottom. "Help me here dude," I ask the frail man as he lifts parts of his anatomy so I can hose the maggots from his red skin. His skin is broken down for some reason, an infection has taken the healthy skin away leaving dead skin for the maggots to feed on. The patient looks down at himself.

"What are those things?" His eyes are wide. "Maggots, they are eating your dead skin, you need to learn to wash yourself out there in the world." The man sits once more on the stretcher, as silence is now the companion between time and water washing. The man is in tears. A sudden feel across the moment is a sorrow of wishes that didn't occur, wants that weren't followed through, in this frail patient's life. "Choices," I say to the man, as I finish washing away the maggots.

Needing a break and it is lunch time after all. The ER has ordered out, I have a good ole burrito waiting for me. Settling into my meal, each bite better than the next, I see the rice. Hmmmm... Why did I get something with white rice on maggot day? Making sure they aren't moving before my next bite, I chomp into it and finish. Of course maggot visuals are in every bite. Diet coke, I need sustenance I grab a cup. The lounge has free fountain drinks for the employee's, although truly it is for the patients. This is another item that will be taken from the ER. Budget cuts, no more cokes or crackers or peanut butter.

Timing is on my side today. As soon as I finish my burrito, the page for a trauma comes over the intercom. Walking quickly back to the trauma room through the main ER, I see Uma, reaching to take a blood pressure cuff off of a patients arm. But this cuff isn't being used to take blood pressure, it is being used to keep an arterial bleed contained until the docs can fix it. I yell at her to stop, but it's too late, she removes the cuff, the blood begins to spurt from the artery that is now exposed.

The patient just laughs as Uma runs out of the room screaming, "help! It's going poof poof," she tosses her hands up with every poof and runs past me. Another tech has already gone into the room with a gloved hand, grabs the arm and asks in anger "what did she do to you?!" The patient just laughs, he wanted to kill himself, he tried by doing the slice of arm thing, so he laughs, Uma almost finished him off.

The trauma room buzzer goes off again, with an added bonus my name is paged all over the ER, because I am late getting to the room. "We need a tech in the trauma room," there is a pause, then added "Jared!"

Uma passes me, her head down, her face red. “Uma, Was ist los?’ She just mumbles “ScheiBkerl (shithead),not sure how to spell it but yea thats what she calls me, it means shit head in German.

Walking quickly back to my trauma room I place the trauma tag on the patient’s ankle but I don’t see any trauma on the man. His shirt is opened, and in a small place in the center of his chest is a dimple. It seems he was working with a nail gun and shot himself in the chest. Moving a ladder he was holding the nail gun and, boom, dead center shot. His vitals suddenly begin to drop, blood pressure, oxygen saturation; his skin begins to get mottled. His skin just doesn’t look right, and he starts to pass out. Before I can even get his temperature, he is rolled immediately out of the room over to the trauma elevators that are near the trauma room to the operating room.

Trauma elevators, you would assume would be fast, not these. They only go to three floors. Yet they take you on a slow ride, all that is missing is elevator music. The patient arrives at the operating room in time to find the head of the nail, piercing the heart with each beat. Causing the heart to bleed slowly and lose profusion.

She came into my trauma room sitting up in all of her elegance on the EMS stretcher. White hair adorns her head followed with a bright smile. She just wasn't feeling right and her vitals were just not good. I tag her and begin the redundant trauma room duties. Roger is the nurse for this lady. Roger has slow blood days at times in the trauma room. He may get the IV in great and fast, but the blood draw is always a painfully slow filling of the blood tubes. He pushes the needle into the ladies arm saying what is always said, "big stick here, don't move." "Ouch!" She yells at him. "I'm sorry," he says as he digs with the IV needle. She retorts, "I know you are sorry but what about your family?" We laugh, she laughs, we talk of casual her skin begins to mottle.

Her profusion is not working, something has gone sour and quickly. She is heading to the Heart Cath lab. As they roll her out, she turns to ask me my name. "You are so nice." Never in my years of trauma has anyone wanted to know my name. I watch them head to the elevators. "What an elegant lady."

I lock up her valuables and had to take the valuable sheet up to the Heart Cath lab to put on her chart. Walking into the lab I see what makes me drop my head and say "no, no, no." A group of docs behind the screen are doing CPR on my sweet, elegant lady.

She didn't come back. I dropped off the sheet with the tech. "No, not my sweet lady".

This hit me in a crooked way. She came into my trauma room with no trauma, she wasn't bloody, she didn't put a gun to her head, her boyfriend didn't try to kill her, she just peacefully rolled in and out..

:::a little furniture stripper please::::::::::::::

He fell into a vat of furniture stripper. I see his body from the belly up is burned red from chemical. I have no idea how this man can survive, surely his lungs are full of the chemical. After a visit to the D'con room, we rush him to the main ER, intubated, hopefully putting fresh air into lungs that are surely messed up beyond fixing. Time does its thing and moves to a moment. He survived with no injuries but the damage to his skin. He passed out before he went head first into the vat and did not breathe in. He didn't breathe at all until he was pulled from the vat. Tada, another moment of ... a very lucky dude.

Another minute, another trauma, "Great one of those stuck in the trauma room, days." I hate these back to back traumas, especially when they come in with a leg on the side. No not fries with that, a leg with that. Drugs and motorcycles don't mix, especially this time, a leg missing and a dude high on cocaine. His right leg is detached from the knee down and EMS is carrying it in. He hands it to me and states flatly "find a home for this." Yea a leg on the side. The bony ripped open side near my blue gloved hand, I have to get a patient valuables bag to put this leg in. This just isn't natural, I think as I shove and turn, and maneuver this limb to find a temporary resting place inside the bag. But it isn't working, watching my blue gloved hands turn the leg, now grabbing the foot. I should have chosen a different job what the hell was I thinking? The hairy limb isn't going to allow itself to be shoved into the not tall enough clothing bag. I improvise and put another bag on top, taping it together. Now where to store the leg, the patient is about to be rushed up to the OR, the leg is not going to be re-attached or he would have it on ice already. But have to keep the parts with the body, maybe there is a warranty?

The patient ready to go, warming blanket on him, a monitor to keep an eye on his vitals, leaves no room to place the leg on top of the stretcher. I put the leg underneath the stretcher with the visual of all of the lost clothing under stretchers daily. I write clearly on wide tape, LEG IS UNDER THE STRETCHER, taping it to the patient's chest. Hoping it will keep the leg from separating further from its owner. I watched as they wheel the patient to the operating room. He is still high on cocaine and feels no pain laughing all the way down the hall.

Without time to stock or even pee, EMS rolls another one in. He was at work and a fork lift truck driven by one of his co-workers crushes him against the wall. He seems ok at first. Pulling off his jeans a surprise is found. He was crushed alright. Crushed a fresh bowel movement right out of him lodged in the pants legs are clumps of turds. “What is this?” Stopping my words in mid sentence, the patient is awake and can see and hear me. Not wanting to embarrass him, I just fold the jeans up after dumping the surprise into the garbage. Some of the turds roll across the trauma room floor.

Somehow this man is ok and away he goes to the CT scan. His loss of bowels kept decently respected. Although some med students chuckled a little as one of the turds did a floor dance.

Much better than a gun spinning away from falling out of a motorcyclists pocket. That was a fun moment, waiting for my foot to be shot. I also had a moment of holy crap, when I thought I was trying to remove a knife from a pocket. Instead I pulled out a gun. I immediately pointed it away from me which then pointed it to all in the room. Oops!

The double doors in the ambulance bay open like clouds dumping held moisture, another trauma literally flies into the room. EMS is doing compressions on this one and he is intubated. I immediately take over CPR.. I push hard and quick on the chest, but feel this man has left the building long ago. His head is crushed, not much of any resemblance of a head is left.

The docs fly into action throwing in the central lines that will send life saving meds immediately into the system. But to no avail. He is long gone, been long gone. The time of death is called and CPR is stopped.

The body bag brought out to prepare the fresh dead for family to view. They will be arriving soon and I will feel their loss, hear their screams and watch them fall to the floor begging just to hear them one last time. To tell them goodbye, to say something they wish they would have said. It is always the same it is always difficult and they are always full of regret.

Before I can get the body ready for the body bag the back doors to the trauma room open and in comes hospital staff with one man. He is put directly across the bay of his dead friend with smashed head. I close the curtains that separate the bays quickly so the man doesn't recognize or know that his friend is lying dead across from him. Staff brought him into the trauma room because he passed out in the hall after hearing that his friend died.

He is quickly assessed and returns to the waiting room. Cindy walks the man back out and glances back at me. Patting me on the back and thanking me for my quick actions she walks out. Cindy is one of those nurses that is special in spirit. At least I think so. She feels the patient's pain and tries to console and truly take care of them.

Putting the fresh dead over to bay four in the trauma room I get ready to feel the possible side affect of pain. It does hit sometimes when least expected. Sorrow, sadness, ripping kind of what the hell feeling, I do not like death.

The story comes in as to what happened. His co-worker and friend were moving some very large pipe using a cable system to haul it to the other side of the warehouse. As his friend was walking under it somehow the piping was dropped on his head.

The family and friends are ushered in. They fall to the floor they cry they scream. But nothing will wake up or bring back their loved one. Nope nothing.

Moving the body to the morgue quickly removing the body and the bag from his stretcher, I toss it onto the cold cart that goes into the cooler. For a moment looking at the room full this day of deads, I feel the temporary of our life here...yea I feel my mortality.

"I think I want a blue body bag, or maybe one with decorations and such?"

My voice trails off as I walk down the long hall in the basement heading back to the main ER. Visuals of decorated body bags for sale now fall into my mind of play. "Maybe I am insane?" One of those flesh people hears me talking to myself. The ones that do the studies on the deads to find out why they died, pathologists they are called.

"Insanity is over rated," she says then smiles at me as I walk past. Nodding in agreement, I just want to go ride my bike or fall into a place of writing, where a story can take me away relieving me of pain. What pain?

Flight is an interesting thing, all want it, they climb high with wings to carry them over and off the mountain cliff. We fly in planes, we fly from reality, when someone pushes that vile of their anger into us. Yea flight is something that I want, away from their pain and my own pain from my past, my life, my walk.

I did the marriage thing, did it for 22 years. The one great reward from the place of, let me spit in your face, was three daughters and a knowing of what true abuse is. It is an insidious creature that spills over the words of love and touch into hatred and anger. Something like mixing shit with ice cream, yea that's what abuse is like. And I had ice cream on a daily basis.

Words are interesting and they mean things and words of anger and control is something I left at the doorstep. I like my little things, writing poetry and stories of short for kids and no anger anywhere near. Yes, flight from the way of pain is an ever constant want into my world. But the grown up thing I have to do is work in the world of normal. Normal is not me in any shape or form. I feel like a handicapped person, trapped, and I will feel this way, unless and until something breaks into my life that has that continued flow and feel of love and comfy I will have to work in the world of pod heads and reality playing the games to walk this place.

-- there is the calm that

comes with love

that love doesn't have to be of earth

it can come from an angels ..sigh

or a light touch of eternity that just happened to slip

from gods fingers....

::
::::

"Get a rectal temperature." Ah the glorious rectal temperature. There is much skill involved in obtaining a rectal temperature without obtaining the bodily fluids or parts of anatomy that sometimes hang down, onto your wrist

I am a right handed rectal temperature getter. Everyone has a good side to putting things in the patients, like foley's, IV's, mine happens to be my right. People don't like having something shoved up their wazoo and when the face is damaged or broken, or they are a head bleed or unconscious, the rectal is a have to be done thing. The rectal technique is different for all but I have the best one. Open their legs just a little, tell the patient "I have to get a temperature in your bottom," is also good to know how to say it in Spanish, which I do.

The fore finger of your weaker hand slides down and into the bottom, slightly the temperature probe is then inserted just beneath the finger, tada, the perfect rectal temperature. Once while training a tech that would be nurse soon, she popped the release of the probe as she was taking the temperature. At least we assume this is what happened.

Well, the bottom likes to pull things up into it, away it went. It was pooped out later we assume? The long and short of it is, getting a temperature in the trauma room is very important, even on a fresh dead, if they die cold, not dead unless warm and dead. Surreal but a happening thing, is getting a temperature on a dead.

The hospital high five, a finger in your bottom, is necessary but most of the patients yell while it's being done. It is to check for tone, or to see if they may have blood in their bottom. Tone is to see if they could possibly be paralyzed. So a finger up the bottom is a medical necessity. If a bottom goes into a trauma room a virgin, it leaves experienced.

When patients are awake and aware but are breathing through their mouth or have on a non re-breather oxygen mask and cold air is blowing over their mouth. The most horrible rectal temperature time occurs. They are going to watch you do it, feel you do it. I tell the lady as she eyeballs me, of a rectal temperature moment. She waits, I push, she says calmly and flatly, "you are in the wrong hole." Red is an interesting color on paper and in art but there is no brighter red than on my face this rectal temperature day.

Women have the other place and at times it is accidentally used. It is still a viable place to get a temperature as is placing the thermometer underneath the balls or, ball, if you will. But when awake and looking at said tech inserting said thermometer with finger pursuing the issue first, it can be a rough moment.

....

The trauma room silent for a moment, cleaned and stocked. I open the doors to the back hall that leads to the trauma elevator. There, in the hall is a stretcher. I dare to lean, to look underneath to see.. and yes I see it, lo and behold the leg from the patient before. Picking up the forgotten leg from underneath the stretcher. I push the button to go to the OR. “Want a leg with that surgery?” I step into the elevator holding a leg, a leg I knew would get lost. “Maybe I have ESP.” The doors open very slowly and close just as fast. The ride is slow up to the second floor, these are the trauma elevators after all, “just need some elevator music and this slow trip would be an escape.” Humming a tune as I ride the elevator to the surgical floor looking down, I see the toes in the bag, I think they wiggled. Averting my eyes quickly I push the button once more to the second floor.

“Nurse!” She screams from her stretcher in one of the bays.

The nurses station, or bar where they mix their ‘cocktails’ ordered up by the docs, is in the middle of the ER. The residents, those almost docs, are on the other side of the ER and somewhere in the middle is the attending’s little spot to park. An attending is a real doctor, getting paid real money, watching the residents learn on real patients. I have watched them grow from first year to third year residents. The hospital does teach them, it takes a true three years, but they are truly ready to rock as doc’s when they leave the hospital, but oh what a ride for the patients up to that point.

“I want something to eat and I want pain meds now, I have been in here for an hour at least and I am starving to death!” I listen to the redundant wish for food and water from yet one more angry patient. “What are you in here for ma’am?” “My stomach hurts real bad, and I can’t stop puking. What is wrong with this hospital, it’s horrible, people treat you like shit, and I am tired!” I don’t even try to interrupt her, “calm down with the yelling ma’am, there are other patients here that are sick.” I turn away from this one as she continues to berate and cut down the hospital.

No matter what is wrong with people they come into the ER and want to be fed. Maybe it's a hospital, hotel confusion in their brains. As soon as I leave the room there is a yell for help at the circle in the back of the ER. A man is lying on the ground in the parking lot near an ambulance. He is badly beaten. Grabbing a wheel chair I head to the man and with one lift pull him into the wheelchair.

I have to hold him in the wheel chair while I push him to the trauma room. The man is mumbling something. Is it about who hit him? Is it about what hurts? No, "I want something to drink I'm so thirsty." Even in the heat and fresh pain people want to be watered or fed. I just smile as I push the trauma button calling all the ones of necessary to the trauma room and help this badly beaten man to a drink of water. Maybe it is a medical condition that occurs when one is beaten or their legs are hanging off their body?

Returning to the main ER after stabilizing the beaten man I look for the nurse for hungry patient to tell them of the want for food, immediately the nurse shoots back, "I have some very sick people on my team, tell them they cannot eat!" Stepping back a bit my hand rises in defense..”whoa lady, don’t shoot the messenger.” Jane calms some and asks forgiveness. “I’m sorry I have three rooms doubled and two patients on a vent.” I nod knowingly, “I know, I know calm down.”

The nature of the beast of this hospital, understaffed, over populated with patients and no bays and sometimes no stretchers for the patients. Suddenly one of the prisoner patients blasts past me knocking me into the counter. The prisoner is running full out for the double ER doors to escape. The problem is the doors are closed and locked by magnets. Everyone leans over the counters and into the hall.

If the ER was a boat at this moment it would have turned over from the weight shift. The vision waiting to behold is the prisoner slamming into the double doors and falling with the same slam to the floor in front of the doors. Flat on his back, timing is everything in life; this guy didn’t have good timing. The doors open slowly as he now rests on his back waiting for security to wrap him up and walk him back to the bay for treatment. Magnets are quite a strong lock for doors. “Fascinating,” is all that I say, the ER recovers from its lean position and continues with duties of drugs and patient care; drawing blood doing EKG’s

....
....

A man of 60's fell...face first, broken nose and the orbits around his eyes and other various facial bones.... he swelled as the day went by...it turns out he has a heart blockage and that's why he passed out. The poor man only wanted to go home... even though he could no longer see through purple swollen eyes filled with blood he wanted to just go home. His dentures were broken inside his mouth and could not be taken out. His fear was huge for this man had only been in the hospital once in his life. Now here he was blinded not knowing what a blood pressure cuff was and scared. I made sure he was clean, got him a hospital bed instead of the stretcher, tried to talk with the family a bit of what was wrong but that's not my place. When I left the room he again just said, "can I go home? I just fell and I wanna go home." Pushing away the feel of his fear I walk to another bay. An interesting man of 92. He didn't look his age at all, I guessed around 60. He was married to a 56 year old. As I was drawing blood from him I accused him of being a cradle robber. He laughed and said he had buried three wives already and that he guesses this one will bury him. We found a room for him quickly and up to the land of hospital he went, away from the ER where the noise and confusion is amazing...

I hear one of the patients crying in one of the beds. "What can I get for you?" She is a middle aged lady, simple in way but with such fear. I can feel her fear, it is like a liquid filling the room and flying into my every thought, I feel it. She looks at me, her eyes wide. “I know I am about to have a seizure I don’t want to have it they scare me.” I walk slowly over to her, standing near her while she lies on the stretcher, “Well I am here to keep you from getting hurt, and your body knows what to do, so just relax and I will be here when you are finished.” She smiles a little, “you are right,” she tries to relax.

Sometimes there are moments that hit me while at work. A moment to reach out and touch a patient, maybe just on their head or shoulder or to give one of those side hugs. This is one of those times. I reach to touch her head. I don’t really reach, I watch my hand reach. It is there in an instant. Now I have to cover this and act like I am just patting her on the head, with the swirl of the room surrounding me my hand touches her head. “You will be ok.” I don’t know what happens when it does, but I believe it happens. I feel as if a small line of energy is coming into the top of my head, through my hand and into her noggin. I write this and feel like they will be coming to take me away to emergency psych. I see things sometimes and this time I see her brain, the energy stilled by this touch of mine. I have no choice, my hand just moves where it is to move.

The room fills with a liquid air, the kind that is thick with a flowing feeling and it feels calm and comfortable. Removing my hand from her head I just smile to cover this awkward moment. "No seizing today little one, not on my watch." I walk out of the room. Glancing back at the patient as the docs walk in to give her meds, she looks at me and I feel her glance to my core, a silent thank you. Re-entering the ER, I feel refreshed and alive with energy, a feel of forever? My thoughts do not question what just happened for it is natural for me to reach for her. Especially when I have no choice. Yea, call the psych people I am surely losing it.

Still in a way of liquid air I walk past another bed, the specialty docs are sewing up a girl's face. It looks like it has been cut like a jigsaw, sliced and gashed. She is underage, but was under the influence when driving, had a wreck, now finds herself in our hospital. The specialty docs want more meds for her. I find her nurse, Mary Lou, usually a good nurse, but today finds her not in a compassionate way. "The docs want pain meds for bed 8." She shakes her head, "I am so busy, do you see how many patients I have, she can wait, she should not have been driving and drinking, I have no compassion for her." I just look at this person, sitting as she looks through her charts, her patients on paper and in the computer. Obviously they are just diseases and broken bones. And if they don't break their bones in an innocent way, she will not give the appropriate meds. Oh no, thou cannot just do ones job.

Have to judge the crack head' the drunk the person of low in life that has to hide inside the halls of drugs or alcohol. Lost for a moment in her lack of, "It is not your place Mary Lou to judge this girl, it is your place to get meds together when the docs order it." She just straightens more papers and starts charting on a different patient. "She can wait and have some pain, I have no compassion for her drinking and driving." I do not know what causes one to feel they can be the god of gods and give medicines when they feel like it. I walk away from this person of non. Frustrated I find another nurse to give the meds to this poor one of pain. With more pain meds on board the docs can finish their patching the quilt that is her face with stitches crisscrossing like a puzzle.

She is a drug addict, she is out of it, she has a crack pipe up her butt. Guess who has to bag it and lock it up? Raising my hand, "me." Another is a lady of the night. She is having abdomen pain, a pelvic exam is done and voila, money is found. Guess who has to lock it up. Money is dirty just passing that on. She came into the ER, something just isn't right. A pelvic is done.

The ER slowly is covered with a stench from a forgotten tampon left inside this lady for weeks.

A yell shatters the ER as EMS brings in what looks like tarzan on an overdose of steroids. The man is huge and his muscles are bulging against the pull of the restraints that EMS has him tied down with. Somehow magically the only thing holding biceps of three feet wide are those triangle scarves used usually in EMS land as slings and such, but most the time they are used as restraints. “Will you help us with this one?” The EMS medic asks me as he walks past pulling the wild man up to a bay. “I spose.” Putting on some gloves and not looking forward at all to messing with this maniac. The patient’s eyes are dashing back and forth and randomly flying up into his head, showing only the whites for just a moment, then dashing his eyes of blue back and forth. As if he is watching a fast and furious tennis match. Security is called to also assist, and the journey begins.

The report slips across in a whisper to the nurse waiting for her new patient. Rita gets the honor. She has been a nurse for many many years, and only works the ER now part time or PRN, which some how means when needed. Rita can handle just about any patient, with a calm and patience the patients feel and usually respect. It seems this mans mother called EMS, because he had decided to rip out the toilet at home and throw it out of the window. She thinks he is possessed, but the reality of it is, he is swinging on steroids.

Security walks into the room to help move the patient from EMS stretcher to ER stretcher. Leather restraints, compliments of the hospital and our wonderful security staff, who has bondage 101 down pat, ready to wrap around wrists that will be attached to the ever growing biceps. I look down at my biceps and glance back at his. I believe this is when distortion came to visit my reality; his biceps were three feet thick.

EMS releases his hands and away he flies, literally. The patient leaps up onto the television set that hangs way up on the wall in the room. Hanging there now like a monkey he climbs further up. Security grabs at him. Rita and I step back out of the room, "These are the best seats Rita, stay by me I have your back." Rita, standing with a syringe ready to sedate the young man, settles near me.

"Sounds like a plan to me," one of the docs smiles as he walks past, "Get this guys blood as soon as they restrain him." Oh great! is my first thought, I get to somehow stick a needle in tarzan here and hope he remains still.

The patient is pulled down hard onto the stretcher. It takes seven of them to hold him down, while the leather restraints are applied to his wrists and ankles. The patient is yelling, cursing, and using words no one has ever heard. Finally done with their job, they file out of the room. I look at Rita, knowing it's time for us to step into the room and begin our duties of the day. She needs to start an IV and give him meds, I need to get his blood.

The resident doc walks in, he is a young one that many of the female nurses and female med students like. It is his boyish quality and muscular body, mixed with soon to be doctor mode, which creates drool moments with the women. I have enjoyed going along on the drug rep parties acting as if I was a med student, which allowed me to enjoy the free meal and free drinks supplied by the drug rep's that are always bribing the docs with such pleasures.

I pushed the Johnny into the patient's room, while Rita and I step out. I am still wondering how I am going to put a small butterfly needle into the huge arms from the amazon to get the needed blood for tests. Rita is wondering how she will get an IV in his amazon arms.

The patient begins to yell again in a language of not known. Johnny walks back out. The patient's mother walks in to see her son. She is very concerned and grabs Johnny. She screams that her son is possessed and needs to have an exorcism. Johnny tries to get the story, and the gist of it is steroids and tossing a good toilet out of the window. He tore up her home, so she called EMS.I watch as he tells her he will do what he can, turning he looks at me with that hidden holy shit look, and walks away from the patient's mother wanting to regroup. She goes into the room and closes the door and the curtains. "Yea let her talk to him maybe calm him down." A small group has now formed near the secretaries desk right outside the bay. His yells are getting louder, and the opinion is formed that obviously mom is upsetting him. I open the door and pull open the curtains.

Moments are crazy in this ER and this was one of movies and monsters. My mind finds the disbelief corner and hides there. The mom has candles lit on the floor, is rocking back and forth mumbling and tossing water onto her son. Her son is livid, thrashing in the stretcher, throwing his head around wildly and pulling at those leathers, with those 8 feet wide biceps. "Security, call security!" Everyone closes on the room while I lift the mom up and blow out the candles quickly. Surprised the place didn't blow up with so much flame and so much oxygen flying around. That is why it is a felony to smoke in a hospital and as I always tell the patients. "Prison time will be offered." The patient begins to laugh maniacally then calls his mother every animal name known to mankind. "He is possessed, he is possessed save me, save me!" Security comes to walk her out to the waiting room; I pick up the instruments of exorcism and cannot help but begin to laugh. Suddenly the patient calms and is just lying there, still.

Dr. Johnny walks back and is now ready to talk with the patient. Vicki, one of the nurses, a cute little woman, small petite frame with short bright golden hair walks up to Johnny and sprinkles normal saline solution on him in the shape of a cross. Rita gets some silk tape and puts a few tape crosses on his scrubs across his chest. "You are ready to go in doc." Vicki says then steps back, we all step back as he approaches the patient's room. He is in there all of three minutes, closes the door behind him and is a bit ashen in color. "I think that man may truly be possessed." He orders meds and IV and walks away in a trance like state. "Yikes," is my first thought, "you go in first." She picks up the phone, "security we need you in bed 4." Rita gets her IV supplies and states with strength, "I'm going in!" The seven stand around him, she tells the patient the facts of IV and that it will happen no matter what. He looks around at all in the room, and settles his stare on me of course. Eye contact is a very personal thing and on this day, this eye contact shot through me like lightning.

“I am going to kill everyone in this room, every last one of you.” Rita doesn’t miss a beat, “well can you wait until I get this IV in first and give you some medicine?” He smiles and relaxes, “deal” but then immediately lifts his head once more, his 8 feet wide biceps flex. His finger tries to point to me, but being kind of stuck to the bed it points to his own foot. “You I will kill first!” I just smile and thank him for the honor. He relaxes once more and yells just as Rita settles to push the needle into his vein. “Get it the first time, or I will kill you first instead of macho over there." This is one of those moments when a tech begins to think of the small amount of money that is paid to work in this ER.

She gets the IV and the blood, I will not have to stick him after all. She hands the blood to me and says “here..” she stops, then finishes, “Paul, take this blood.” Standing still for a moment, I look around wondering who is Paul. She winks and it becomes clear, “Oh yea, thanks Mary Jane.” Walking quickly out of the room, under my breath, “the names have been changed to protect the innocent.”

Quickies...::

She was cooking bacon, talking on the phone and drinking coffee. She turned to take one last gulp of her coffee, she drank the hot grease instead. Not fun coffee memory.....

An elderly couple arrives at the emergency room. I show them to their room, Bed 1. I get him into a gown, but he cannot sit down. Lying on his side on the stretcher I leave. Glancing back I cannot help but shake my head. They were playing around sexually and decided to see what a can of corn shoved up his butt would feel like to him. Well, it's stuck.

The bottom does not like to let go of things put up into it. It's a fact. He came from another part of the state, a police officer. He is lying on his side. A pipe is stuck up his butt. Surgery will leave him with a colostomy for months. I say "huh?" Do you want fries with that?

She called the ER frantic, "help I have a question?" I tell her I cannot give medical advice out over the phone. But, they never listen. Somehow all of their ills will be cured over the phone. "Let me just tell you!" I say ok. "I lost my dildo and thought I left it up inside myself. So I got some hemostats and used them to reach up and pull at what was left up there." My mouth fell open, she continued. "I started to bleed, but kept pulling and ripping something apart." My mouth shut. "Then I saw the dildo sitting on the coffee table." "Um.." I say slowly. "What should I do? Do you think I'm hurt?" " You need to come to the ER and get checked out. I hang up the phone.

She calls with that scared tone in her voice. "I need help what should I do" "I cannot give out medical advice..etc etc" "My mother is a diabetic and her sugar is 20" "Call 911, give her orange juice and sugar now!" She hangs up. I'm sweating, what the hell?

A young man is rolled into the main emergency room. He broke his penis It is bent and broken. His story is, he rolled over in bed and "he broke his penis/unit" Cough/bullshit/cough...

Another young man is rolled in. Must be bent dick day. He tells of having hard sex with his woman and missing after a withdraw, then slamming into her. Wham! broken.. (ouch).

Two men, doubled in a room on two stretchers. One is a Hispanic speaking man of youth, the other is English speaking white male. The younger Hispanic one watches as the docs examine the patient next to him. The body has to be exposed when they check for trauma on the legs, hips, chest etc. The man happens to be well endowed in the unit arena. I glance at the other man, as he looks down at his penis, then looks over at the other guys penis, obviously comparing the two. His is much smaller. The younger man has a foley catheter in his. He was unconscious for a time and it had to be put in.

Possibly he had no idea what that tube was in his penis, and he thought it was draining him of his size? I have no idea, but five minutes after we walk out of the room. I see the nurse, lean outside the room peeking through the curtain asking for help. I walk in; the young one is standing naked facing the toilet in the room. His back is to me. I see blood pouring out of him onto the toilet and to the floor. He is holding his penis in one hand and the catheter in the other. He pulled out the catheter, they have a small balloon inflated inside to keep them in the bladder. He has just ripped out any chance of ever getting erect again.

I mean, seriously?

The husband dies suddenly, the wife is not around for comment. Her eyes are blank, she won't leave the room. She holds his hand, she talks to him, she holds his hand. This bothers me, I walk away....

I am asked to help get a fresh dead ready for the morgue. No family around, just bag it and roll it to the morgue. I had just received my shining star award and there I go be-bopping up to the sheet covered dead body. Never approach an unknown dead body and lean to see what needs to be cleaned up. I lean, pull the sheet back, and almost pass out in pure fright, fear, horrible moment emotion. He…it, was intubated, so the tube is sticking out of his mouth. His lips have been pulled back by the string they use to tie the tube in place. His mouth is wide open, teeth exposed. His pupils are blown, which means huge black center and the whites of his eyes are bloodshot. So imagine the worst monster attack facial moment and that is it. Barely dropping the sheet over his face I ran out of the room. I was then called "the shooting star". Not returning to that room. Nope, someone else had to do it.

Inventions are an amazing and wonderful thing created out of necessity. A butt bag is a feeble attempt at an amazing invention. A man is intubated, the machine is breathing for him, but he continues to create loose stool. It is butt bag time. Donna asks for my help to prepare this young ones butt for the procedure. Pam, another tech, comes in to help. We roll the patient, spread his butt cheeks allowing Donna to shave his butt cheeks with a dry razor. She then applies butt glue. Yes glue to a freshly shaved bottom. Pam is holding the patient on his side. I am holding one leg up, while Donna gently spreads the cheeks to apply the 'butt glue'. He instantly clamps down, "Don't do that, you will glue your butt together" She pulls open the cheeks, I am still holding the leg up some and Pam is holding him to his side.

While we wait for said glue to dry, we converse. “What are you doing tonight?” Conversation continues as I realize we are having a butt campfire conversation. Casual of convo over a dudes butt hole waiting for glue to dry. Not right.... The bag is applied, the poop will be captured. Another good deed done, with an amazing invention called a butt bag. They have new ones now that are inserted into the bottom. Didn’t have those back in my days.

::::::

Heading to the break room I have to walk past one of the nurses I have a crush on. But she is unaware of my desires. Although being a poet, artist, martial artist and one of life and such, I enjoy many aspects of women. So today I may have a crush on one of the residents and tomorrow they are just, one of the residents. This current want is a new nurse that has decided to join the fun in the emergency room. No one glances my way, anyway, at least in that way of potential or possible to be with into that eternity place kind of glance.

Partly because I never show anyone too much of my depth and partly because I am used to the nurses glancing past me to the handsome doctor or the potential money maker. Doctors should just be called money-tors. My life of women and love is outside of this ER and this reality. Maybe it is the familiar day to day energy exchange that messes it up for most people that work together. The work place becomes like that of a family. One may talk with a most beautiful nurse that has all the sensuality that normally knocks me off my feet in the real world. But in my place of work, my ER, she is just a nurse. I have a few that I went through the lust for phase. But it eases into the just the person I work with phase.

She is a new nurse to the ER, came from the med surge floor in the hospital, but is a cute thing, according to me anyway. She wears her hair wrapped around in swirls, jet black hair, teasing anyone near it to untie it from its hold and watch the cascade of shine fall down, past her shoulders. Her eyes of light blue contrast her beauty, her skin, oh her skin. My thoughts find my mouth against her skin. I walk past what I know will never even glance my way yet alone allow my mouth near any part of her heaven. I am having one of my pitiful moment days. Feeling a little less than good enough for anyone, divorced and old at the age of fifty two, hustler of pool, an old martial artist that writes goofy sentimental poetry, top that off with "just a tech" and tada you have the perfect no interesting type person all wrapped in one bundle called Jared.

Uma walks into the lounge, cursing in German. She grabs a cup, fills it with diet coke, gulps it down then walks out as quickly as she came in. The German is in an uproar.

The trauma buzzer sounds once more. Grabbing gloves from the cart outside the door to the room, the flurry of docs and specialty teams, all reach for gloves as they parade into the trauma room, X-ray close behind.

He was ejected from his car. He landed on a fence. He came in with the post through his body. Still alive, we don't do much with him but get him to the OR. The board is thick through his midsection, and just doesn't look right.

She was under the influence, she is a mother who had a passenger riding with her in the car, it was her daughter, she is dead.. I watch them tell her the news of this death. The officer is near the room. She screams with sorrow, she will go to jail.

He is a young man in the hospital after a night of drinking with his friends. He wakes up asking about his friends. I watch them lean to tell him they are all dead. He is the driver, they are dead, he will go to jail.

The trauma doors burst open once more.

Blood is released from a fresh bullet through the head, a self inflicted act of waste. Keeping the patient alive to make sure CODA can't use the parts is all that is done at this point. The hole in the back of his head is pretty large, large caliber bullet, leaves large exit wound. Everyone seeing the blood splattering onto the floor from the back of this guys head turn and get the yellow gowns. The yellow gowns are good at keeping blood off the cool black scrubs and also keeps one warm in the ER.

I begin to stare at the amount of blood now accumulating onto the floor around the stretcher. IV fluids are still moving into this guy to hydrate his organs, but the fluids have to go somewhere and they are literally spraying his blood out onto the floor. Grabbing some sheets and towels to toss onto the never ending red sea, hoping to stop the flow, but to no avail. "Look guys, you are making a mess here, stop the bleeding." Looking at the docs, I point to the obvious blood covered floor, the response? "We are waiting on the OR, have to keep fluids moving through him to save the other organs." Finally they leave the trauma room. Leaving the leaky patient with me. I push him into bay 4, the bay where the fresh deads are usually kept, for family to see after they are cleaned up and at least a little presentable.

Wrapping a towel around the mans open head, I try to make a turban to stop the flow some. Family is soon to come and view the body, the family was there when he shot himself. Nice gift to your loved ones. So now it is time to say goodbye, as the perpetual leak of blood forms to the right side of the stretcher. I call the chaplain in to stand on that side of the stretcher so the family doesn't have to see the blood from their loving father drip blood onto the floor or onto them.

In they walk, I can hear the dripping of blood. I look at the family wondering if they hear it also. They are too busy crying and yelling at him for doing such a thing. "Whew." Thelma walks in behind me, "do you need me in here yet?" I had closed the curtains around the original bay, I pointed to the curtains, which remained closed so the family wouldn't see. "Clean up in aisle bay one." She walks over to the curtain and slowly pulls it back, "oh my god!" she says before she can stop the words. The family turns to see her and unfortunately see past her. As the daughter begins to cry, "Look that's daddy's blood, look momma!" Thelma closes the curtains quickly and leaves to get her cleaning supplies. The chaplain walks the family away from the trauma room hitting me on her way out, throwing me a look of cover up the blood next time!

The chaplains do miracles at this ER. They are the go between with the families and the docs. They comfort, arrange for care, offer drinks and make everything ok. I love me some Kathy. She is my favorite chaplain. She is an angel straight from the rays of God's smile. She comforts and truly has a healing gift with the families. Lisa is another one, she could be Kathy's sister angel partner in chaplain lands.

I smile at her and shoo her from the trauma room. As they walk out of the back of the trauma room and Thelma begins her mopping of the massive blood splat on the floor, the doors fly open once more.

The nurse, David, a big strong dude, carries the guy in and throws him on the stretcher in bay 2. I am told to start CPR, and away the docs fly. The nurses move around the patient getting the drugs out that are ordered quickly. I continue my compressions on the blue from the shoulders up dead dude. Yea the man is blue from the shoulders up, dropped dead while being triaged into the ER. They hit him with all the heart failure drugs, ,

The resident orders all to get back, ready to shock. "I'm clear, you're clear, we're all clear, clear!" Wham! 200 Joules of electricity slams into his body. He almost sits up with the shock, his body lifts higher than any of them have ever seen. "Wow," is all I can get out. My arms already pumped from doing the chest compressions, I just wait for the order to continue CPR. A few more pushes and the docs order once more for a shock. Wham, they hit him again, he rises even higher than the first time.

One of the docs says in a whisper to me, “wow, just like on TV,” suddenly the patient starts to talk, saying how he has just not felt right, he stops in mid sentence looks around the trauma room and asks, “where the hell am I?” The doc proceeds to tell him that he was dead, and we brought him back. The room calms the meds are in, the patient is alive once more. I have never, in all of my years working the ER, ever seen anyone come back like that from a full arrest. They have come back to have a heart beat but they have brain damage or it’s just long enough for their family to prepare for their death.

The doc that handled this one is a little strange, but brilliant, “well that’s why we come to work isn’t it, my my, look at that.” He walks out of the room, the patient is wheeled over to X-ray and I have yet another mess to clean up. “Thelma look,” I flex my freshly pumped biceps and Thelma just shakes her head, “you wear me out," she says to me then smiles.

The doors fly open once more, a lady is sitting up in the stretcher, but the right side of her neck is wide open and flapping as she turns to look around the room. The patient with open flap neck is a lady that decided she wants to die. Numbed her neck appropriately with that numbing stuff and her wrists, used a razor to hack away at her throat and her wrists. Why is she alive? Suddenly many are made to leave the trauma room, turns out she is the wife of one of someone important in the hospital on another floor. Shhhhhh, is the word, no one is to know of this, shhhhh, which of course shoots a flurry of whispers across the ER and through the whole hospital. People will always be people.

I still cannot believe the way her neck looks. It is hanging open with jagged edges and flapping as she talks. The docs look into her neck and are a bit lost in what to do. I ask one of the docs why she isn't dead, why is her neck wide open like that. The doc says it's a miracle, for she clotted some how, now how to repair the damage to that artery. Other nurses and techs wander in to see the injury, this is a teaching hospital after all. They are scurried away, but I get to stay in and watch the drama of the important person, husband, finding his nurse wife with her neck half cut away in front of his peers. She tells him of her love for him, but then tells of how she saw the blood and knew she did it right but then she stopped bleeding, but she was too doped up to move to cut herself more. Watching in amazement I do not understand, she has money, she is beautiful, she is married, why is she hacking away at her neck?

They are very cautious as they look inside her neck. She is moved quickly to the OR. There are people in this place of time and wishes that I feel they are here test to others. Spirits or lights of good, whatever name they are real, they come to mind as they sacrifice a small amount of time living in flesh on earth to test the pod heads of life. His name is Ralph and he is homeless. He is also an alcoholic. His redundant visits to the emergency room create and attitude of disgust with most. EMS tosses his limp drunk body around on the stretcher as they wait to triage him into the ER. “Hey Ralph wake up.”

I met Ralph for the first time on a morning crazy as usual in the ER. Ralph has to go to the d’con room, in other words he smells bad and has left over waste still on his body. I am asked to take him and give him a shower. I use the d’con room to shower him and get him smelling good enough for all around him to tolerate his presence. Ralph was a gentle soul, his eyes just about knocked me back with just a glance. Ralph had a light inside him that was more than bright it, was in the brilliant category. Either he was an angel or a test or just a choice made before his birth to live this life testing those that walk life to see how they will treat a soul of no money and of dirty clothes. I saw Ralph just hours before he was found dead in a park near the hospital. He was walking away from our hospital without any shoes on. I stopped him, told him to keep walking and that I would meet him at the front of the hospital. I got some of our lost shoes then ran to meet him. I made him sit down, while I put the shoes on his feet. As he stood he thanked me, "where are you going now Ralph?" He started to walk slowly away from me, "To find someplace to sleep".

That was the last I saw him alive. I went to his funeral.

More::::::

Finished with another trauma I try to get back to the main ER to help with the small tasks such as emptying the soiled linen carts. But as soon as I begin to lift the first bag of the soiled linens into a cart, the trauma buzzer goes off again.

A young lady is rolled into the trauma room. Her neck is cut wide open. Someone tried to cut off her head with garden shears. He took her to a park to kill her and her children. The kids got away. She got away. She tries to talk, but just gurgling sounds are heard as blood rolls out of her opened neck. I run to get blood, they take her away quickly to the OR. I don't think she will live.

I was working triage a week later. A patient walks in with a bandage on her throat. She has to get it checked. I'm thinking wound check for first care, then I realize it is that lady and she is alive! I tell her of my side of the story of her walk into our trauma room. She thanks me for being part of the team that saved her life.

A GSW arrives, gun shot wound. Nine bullet holes, to be exact.. The docs call the time of death, Dr. Hadley, the attending for the day, who is a very well known doctor, having been published in medical journals and books across the US, begins to take pictures of the victim of gun shots for his medical book. The death paper work has begun, the rush has slowed, another dead in the trauma room, it happens often. I open a fresh body bag to bag this fresh dead, but I see his chest moving. He is breathing? Nine minutes after this man stops breathing and is called, dead he decides to breathe again. His chest rises, one of the nurses says, "I see him breathing?." Dr. Hadley taking pictures concurs that he is breathing and just shakes his head.

The haste begins once more as they turn on all the monitors and talk to the man, the man that was dead for nine minutes. No profusion, no oxygen given to him, nothing but here he is breathing and now talking. Not remembering anything, he is sent to the OR, but slowly, for his vitals are great, he is awake he is alive. A miracle most say. He doesn't remember anything about the shooting or being dead and he is as if nothing happened, a fine healthy young man.

The doors fly open once more bringing in another miracle man into the trauma room. His car broke down on the interstate and he was trying to cross the interstate to the shoulder on the road. But instead of an easy walk he was hit by a car that was traveling 70 miles per hour, rode the top of the car for a time then was tossed to the pavement. EMS presents him to our trauma room. He is talking, he is collared and on a back board but he shows no sign of trauma.

Dr. Hadley comes into the room to begin his evaluation. Nothing is found. The man is laughing and talking telling of his flight in time. They do not keep him in the trauma room he will be rolled out to triage then sent to the main ER just to make sure they haven't missed anything. Dr. Hadley asks before he leaves the room. "What happened again son?" He tells of seeing the car coming toward him and he jumped up as high as he could. The car instead of smacking him with full impact hits him with a glancing blow? "You need to buy a lottery ticket young man you are one lucky person." The boy is released a few hours later with absolutely no injuries. Miracle man? Nah, spirits at work. This dude wasn't supposed to get hurt today.

The memory of my own moment of not supposed to get hurt, I was at my Dad's house for Christmas. My nephew Eric was in front of me as he ran up the back stairs to the house. Eric held the back door open to allow me to go into the house first. Somehow in my elegance of run up the stairs, I tripped. I can still see my right hand pushing to catch myself on the stairs. But my hand open and spread waiting to take part of the blunt of the trip never touched the stairs. I was held somehow in the air for just a moment then let down with an easy klunk. My nephew yelled, "man you just did a matrix thing you were in the air!"

So, yea, I know of those days of not supposed to get hurt. Blame it on luck or thick air but sometimes teeny miracle things happen.

School was a place of torture for me. With uncomfortable uniforms and teachers that would rather be yelling than teaching. Lunch and recess were the favorite times of the day. Standing with my 30 cents ready for my milk and delicious potato sticks. On the lucky days when my mom was there to help serve the lunch I hoped to get extra. But no, she gave me the regular scoop as all the other kids got. Flying out into the playground I was free from the walls of torture. Imagination is flight and I knew how to fly. Thoughts of the words of religion taught that day also found my recess moments.

Attending a Catholic grade school gives in to a different kind of torture. Mass daily. My thoughts would try to discern the reality or the common sense of what was said in the holy word thing. I didn't understand how I shouldn't steal money for my candy habit or not live forever in heaven. I had to think long and hard on that one. Having a talk with, "The Big Guy," I decided that yes I did not want to burn forever in a place called hell. But a compromise would have to be found. Because I did need my candy and I would continue to steal to get it. I asked with my eyes closed and all my heart for a ticket to go to heaven. I just knew I would never make it without help. After I asked for that ticket I felt I was good to go. The rest of my day was of play, I had a ticket to ride, to the heaven place.

.

::

Listening with ears of silence

..opens the deepest caverns of silence   echoing into our hearts..

a whisper   of   love

--

The main ER is piling up with people, every room is doubled which doesn't leave much room. In one of the bays there is a man with obvious turrets syndrome yelling. Turrets syndrome is an interesting illness that causes people to curse or have peculiar tics, uncontrollable tics. Next to this man cursing suddenly in bursts, lays a kind old man from a nursing home. He is very upset with the language being presented, "Are you ok sir?" I walk in to try to comfort him. The turrets patient continues with his rant of inappropriate words, "cock sucker, shit face, face, face," he twitches as well. I tried to calm the guy by touching his arm and telling him he will be ok. Handing him the call button was the only thing I could give him. Walking out of the bay the cursing continues, looking back I see the old man cringe.

Down the hall is a drunk still on a backboard, yelling "I have to poop!" along with this now chorus of yells in the emergency room comes a reply from another patient, a druggie responding to his yells, "well go ahead,' his reply "Sarah?" "No she left your sorry ass," standing for a moment, I listen as the three voices seem to start a song of a very odd nature. "Cock sucker, shit face,face, face," "I have to poop," "go ahead poop," "Sarah?" "No she left your sorry ass." "Cock sucker shit face, face." The cycle doesn't slow until I go to the guy on the backboard. "Sir I can put you on a bedpan, but you can't get off the backboard." The smell of alcohol is strong , "No! I will just wait." He yells and I walk out the voices continue their song. It is almost time to go home and the day has worn me down.

The pretty nurse is finishing putting together some more meds. I just watch her for a little bit. All of the women in my past flash like cards across my brains eyeballs.

I have a gift of giving, and it seems most women don't understand why they feel me so deeply and run away. They find someone else pretty quickly, giving them love and comfort and trust. Everything I want from them, but just don't seem to get. I am doomed in life to just show women how to love, and then let them fly to another. One of my favorite poems, for it seems to suit my life.

::::

there is a spot the size of forever..

.it sits upon my shoulder trying to find a life...

the fuel of her fire has been removed

now he will have what I showed her he will feel

what I gave her...there is a spot that I will place

into another.. then I will have.... forever

:::::

The night shift begins to walk in looking like a long line of zombies, awake barely and stiff in stride. Tired from the day, and tomorrow I return, 12 more hours of? A tech is nothing in the way of work, barely pays and is very hard work..

..........::::

Drinking wine is fine..

sipping the air is a delight..

finding tomorrow I am alive..

finding romance ..

never dies:::

......

Suddenly the daughter of one of the patients comes out of her mother's bay. Calling for people to come. Her mother is very close to dying, "Look at her she needs some meds or something." The daughter walks over and picks at her mother's skin, then putting whatever she picks off of her into her mouth. "I will get your nurse, she will help." She nods and continues to pick at pieces of her mother, pulling off scabs, tasting then popping them into her mouth.

A wave of nausea falls across my gut over this.. “Ma’am maybe you should wait out in the waiting room for a bit until we get your mother settled.” The nurse for this room walks up, “what’s wrong Ms. Johnson?” I just step away from this lady she isn’t natural.

The daughter tells her concern, but all the while she picks at her mothers skin. The mother’s pressure is dropping, all of her vitals are not good, and she will not be alive long. The nurse tells the daughter she can be with her just a little longer then she will have to leave. She closes the curtain for her to be with her for some alone time. “Did you see her?” Leaning to whisper to the nurse, she agrees with me. “She is a nut case,” pulling back the curtains I see something that should never be seen on any world of worlds. Pulling the catheter away from the daughter. The catheter that she is sucking on, sucking her mothers urine out of the catheter that was just inside her mother’s bladder. She ripped it out and was sucking the urine out of the tube. A moment of hurl hits me. Good thing I am Shao-Lin warrior, I would have lost it then. Her mother is dead, the words from the daughter as she is being taken away, “Can I go to the morgue with you?” A moment of done, done, done, I was done with this day.

--

Silence of beauty

…is that one moment

when the air mixes with

your inhale..

flowers know the secret to rise

trees know the way to survive

..but the air has the power

to involve…..me in the life

of ..beauty

John a night tech is assigned the trauma room; John is an interesting fellow, once a stand up comedian now a tech working towards being a nurse. Freshly married and now a father, I have watched him grow in the medical world. John is one of the good guys, he genuinely cares for the patients and will treat them with respect, no matter what they spit at him, and he is always polite and calm on the return. And if you come in with a full arrest and John is on duty, your heart will have no choice but to beat. I have never seen such hard compressions done by anyone, John makes it look easy.

Erin, a young blonde happy type nurse, walks up to us and hits me on the arm. "Going out for beers tonight with the group?" Therapy night is what it should be called. Sometimes when the day is full of death, anger, blood, and maggots, a group will meet after work to talk of the day and complain or laugh about the patient's or another nurse or tech. This is the only time I can talk about my job while eating. Truly, it is the only time I can talk of my job. Friends and family never want to hear of the brains exposed or brain matter on the floor or oozing out of someone's nose. But my peers flinch not. I really just want to go home. But will make a sacrifice for the masses. I agree to the beer and the convo.

My report given to John I walk to my locker. I am tired. My shears dropped back into their hold in the locker I turn to see myself in the mirror. A tired looking soul, grey hair messed up a little, blue eyes show some sadness. Leaving to catch up with all that are heading to unwind, I walk past the stretchers in the back hall. Some still with blood fresh on them. How many have died on those stretchers. We place our badges against the gate keeper or the time clock, same thing. "Transaction accepted," the computerized voice, signals all is well and we may now leave..

The ER is getting louder, and the ambulances are piling up bringing more than the ER can hold, but that is the nature of the beast at this hospital.

Outside.:::::::::

Walking outside, the fresh night air feels good, cool but good. It is the used to be happy time of December, and Christmas is near. Maybe my kids will want to do something of a family thing this year. Maybe not.

My van is at the middle of the parking lot. Looking down at my feet walking, black boots I have worn when I was an EMT, moving across black pavement, into the black night. “Now I am thinking poetically.” The image of that lady sucking on a urine filled catheter doesn’t seem to want to leave my mind very quickly.

The lady with the open neck and the images of abuse, my mind will not release the day’s images just yet. My van sturdy and old a 1993 Chevy Astro, EXT. I like the power and the size of the van, plus, in a pinch one can live in it. I am too tired to do the after work social gripe session. The night is my companion. Heading to my apartment, my rented place of life and living. My kids are on their own and gone with their own perspective versions of paths with choices mixed in.

::::::

: water falls hold more than moisture::

little ones have magic..with a faery

mixed in::

::::::::::

The Next Day::

If alarms where alive, it would be slapping me senseless, but this alarm with its shallow beep, beep, beep, falls into my dreams. Everything unplugged in my dreams, but the sound is still there. I run in my dream, to every machine, pulling plugs but to no avail. Finally waking enough to slap off the alarm and rolling out of my bed that lies on the floor. No box springs, nada, just the top mattress, I have a difficult time standing. "I need a grown up bed." The hard wood floors are cold to my feet as I stumble into the bathroom. Another day another patient cursing at me, spitting on me, swinging at me, gotta love it.

My place of current living is a duplex. It is comfortable and small, two bedrooms, one bathroom with a shower tub and a toilet that sits facing a wall, a mere one foot away. As I get ready to hit the day again my words as they always do find the air.

Talking to myself has become a daily routine. "Who will die this day, do you know you will die?"

She was crossing the road, she was hit by a car. Her leg tossed to the floor of the trauma room. Her right arm hanging by mere tendons off of the stretcher. Her muscles spun from the tear of her leg off and away. I look at the shoe that still contains a foot now shrunken because the fluid has left its home with blood surrounding the once white tennis shoe. She is dead. Her toe nails freshly painted, young lady in her early teens, brain dead and a Jane Doe. No one to call, No one to tell, I was to draw her blood for a test. Her body still, on a vent that is breathing for her, her hair long and blonde flowing down onto the white sheets of the stretcher. The silence in the room and the stillness of this girl still flies against my thoughts, her toe nails painted red, her body dead, alive only by the air we force into her lungs.

'Who will die today.' The parking lot is filling up with the morning shift, My ID card pushed against the gate box, to allow entrance. That beautiful sunrise finds my eyes once more. The Van turns into a slot and the day soon begins. The air is colder this morning than the night, My P-coat pulled closed, hands in pocket, black scrubs and black boots watching my feet move across that familiar black pavement. Who will die today, I envision someone getting ready for work. Neatly applying their makeup or cologne, pulling up their hose or socks, slipping their feet into heels or boots, the flash then finds my trauma room, Their body broken, blood leaving at will, bones slipped and escaping their home. Home, flashes a feeling of peace into his core, for now they are dead and released to home.

The door opens to the ER, the clock is waiting, the gate keeper. Badges placed against, 'transaction accepted'. The computer voice now greets all day shift for 12 hours of most likely hell.

My locker awaits, opening it slowly, sitting on the bench that is in front of my locker. Leaning I try to visualize a good day, all working well and no death. Removing my P-coat, placing it into my locker. I find my trauma shears. It feels like I just put them in there, but that was a mere 12 hours ago.
Time keeps on slippin .....

The assignment board is a white dry erase board where all of the action begins. The charge nurse writes on the board which room the techs and nurses will have.

Today I have triage in the morning and the trauma room the second half of the day. I love early triage, it's usually easy. People seem to sleep in late then decide they need emergent care later in the day.

Triage is an animal in itself. The tech sits at the front bullet proof glass window. This hospital is in the middle of downtown Mayville, bullet proof glass is a needed precaution. Security also searches all that walk in through the back ER doors.

The night tech is ready to get out of triage. It seems it was not a good night, many patients waiting to get back to a full ER. Not a good thing when taking over triage. All of the angry sick people will be coming up to yell at me and ask when they will get back to be seen.

Juan begins to walk away from me shaking his head, "good luck, they are angry." Juan is a Spanish speaking cool dude. He sells real estate on the side. All of the techs working at this ER have second or sometimes third jobs, because the tech pay is horrible. The hospital expects you to enjoy the benefit of seeing everything and anything under the sun, hence that is your payment.

The sick walk begins and it isn't even 7:30, they walk slowly with a lean toward the window. It's kind of scary at times. "Can I help you?" My voice barely heard through a small vent looking circular silver thing they have put in the center of the bullet proof glass. “I need to get back to see my mother right now!” “Last name please?” People are usually very nervous, upset and angry when they come to the hospital. One thing they always forget is the last name of their loved one. Asking this question stirs them to anger slap me with her body language and the tone in their voice. “Darwin." She looks away cursing the ER to another patient waiting to sign in. “Room five, c’mon in.” I push the button that unlocks the door, she walks in with anger tossing me a look of fuck you, and walks to the back towards the main ER.

“We need a wheelchair now!” A lady screams as she leans into the microphone at the window. ‘My boyfriend cant walk, can’t talk.” I try to find a wheelchair, something else this hospital is short of. They are stolen on a regular basis. Luckily on this day there is one in triage. Unlocking the door I push it out to the ER circle. Cars can pull up in a semi circle to drop off emergent patients. There is a man in a car, unresponsive to my attempts to awaken him. The hospital has communicators that you wear around your neck, with one push of a button you can call all of the employees for anything wanted, either to get lunch orders or for this time to get help with an unresponsive patient. I call immediately for help in the ER circle.

But this guy is not breathing, no pulse, he is dead in the car. Lifting him the best I can, trying to act like my old EMS days I throw him in the wheelchair and attempt to do CPR on a patient in a sitting position.

Making it to the trauma room, all quickly show up giving me a break on the compressions. Standing back I watch the staff work this dead guy. Attempting to bring him back to life, but it isn't working.

Humor is interesting in a morbid way at times in the emergency room. All begin to chuckle slightly, softly, trying not to laugh at the sight. Meaning no disrespect but it is difficult to remain serious when doing CPR on a naked man when with every push on the chest his penis takes a flop into the air. As his chest drop occurs it drops also. Uma is laughing so hard she is barely pushing. All are fixated on this dead mans unit. It flops up and down with each push. Finally the time of death is called. The penis full of life is now stilled. It had one last bit of flight? Uma is red but cannot stop laughing. Patting her on the back I just smile. "You devil you, look what you did to him!" She says something in German but smiles.

The line at the triage window has grown and now stretches almost out of the door into the parking lot. Sign in sheets are being flung through the window, as one after the other sign in and toss it into the small opening at the bottom of the bullet proof glass. A lady runs up to the window and begins pounding on it. "My son, my son is here!"

I have seen much death, watched the brain matter fall out onto the stretcher from fresh gun shot wounds or a blow to the skull. I have turned the dead and watched the pink foam find its way through the nostrils. I see this woman afraid, panicked beyond any day she has ever had. She is at my window and is about to have the worst day of her life.

Calmly asking the name, I am given just a first name. "Tom!" Waiting for what will never occur unless I ask for it, the last name.

He is in the trauma room, so I have to show her to the special waiting rooms. These rooms are more private, giving the doctors a chance to talk with the family on the condition of their loved ones without people watching or hearing the news.

This alone causes a freak out moment, for they just know you are going to give them bad news. I have always called them the bad news rooms. They took us into one when my mother was gravely ill. It was very small. I knew it was to keep the screaming inside the walls and not to bother other people at the hospital.

I begin my speak to the family as to why they have to go to the little waiting room. I tell of the protocol when patients are in the trauma room, that the chaplain will be notified, as a go between for the family and the docs.

Watching them walk into the small room, their fear seems to fill the whole room. Turning away from this emotion, something I want no part of nor can do anything about. I walk back to the ever growing hell hole called triage. They file in as if a bus has let out somewhere down the road. The emergent nature? "I just don't feel good." The usual response. ER abuse yea, that's the ticket.

Triage on the tech end consists of getting yelled at by angry patients waiting for hours to get back to the main ER, getting vitals, making sure they are not suicidal or homicidal. If they are HI or SI, hospital code for the two, then you have to make sure they do not leave your sight until security walks them to Psych. The psych department is supposed to triage their own, somehow they have the power to just say no, which leaves the tech at the window in a very vulnerable position. Psych patients are not always nice, many are violent and mostly uncontrollable. In the triage area it is wide open with the 'normals' that walk through.

Psych has a small room where they are able to keep the patient close and under supervision, but do they do that?

I thought one day as I worked this triage animal that the aliens were working the human types. Eight people in a row complained of the same ailment, they went to sleep with feeling ok and woke up with back ailments, all had the same ailments, go figure.

Vitals started on a fresh patient. He has put down he is hearing voices. A very good sign that he needs to ask if he is SI or HI, "you hear voices?" The young guy nods. The patient's eyes are glazed over and his body twitches. "Do you want to kill yourself?" "No," a monotone response is given, "do you want to kill someone else?" "yes everybody." I note this on the sheet then look him in the eyes. "Can I get your vitals first before you kill me?" The guy lifts his head and smiles, then starts to laugh some. Putting his arm up so that I can put on the blood pressure cuff, "Sure I will wait," he laughs again and calms some.

I can feel this mans confusion, I see the light the mix and the crooked corners in his soul. I look straight into his eyes, "we will help you dude, no worries ok?" The man relaxes in a physical way and a spiritual way. But it is only a moment. Feeling the tension build again as the patient decides he wants to leave now and not be seen. Now we have the scenario of a trapped animal. The triage door is locked and the guy who wants to kill everybody wants to leave. “Can’t let you go yet,” somehow, this time he relaxes.

There is a new nurse working triage, the nurses finish the triage moment by asking more detailed questions and putting the patient in the computer, and hopefully into a room in the ER. This new nurse is on her first day alone at triage. New nurses at triage, horrible and slow.

I walk the guy over to her desk, put the triage sheet down and tell her he is HI. I look at her with the look of “don’t let him out of your sight.” She begins to ask him questions, she then asks, “are you suicidal or homicidal?” The guy just says “no.” She looks at me and shakes her head. Why did you mark this down here! “She begins to draw a line through what the patient stated to me. I walk over to the guy, lean closer to him, “do you want to kill anyone,” he smiles and raises his head, “yes, and I will kill you after she is done, with triaging me,” he laughs harder. New nurses!

There are times in triage when something from the lands of cannot believe occur. They walk up to the window. Two elderly ladies with their brother in a wheelchair. “Please help us.” I look at the guy in the wheelchair. This guy looks not well. Standing I open the door, “come in ladies and gent I will help you with the paper work.” They push the older man through the door. The wheelchair barely fits.

This guy looks horrible. “I will get your vitals sir, what are you here for today?' I ask while putting the cuff on the old guys arm. One of the sisters begins to tell the story. “Well we just can’t get him to eat.” The other one of follows as if to finish the sentence, “He won’t move out of the chair and he won’t talk to us,” she steps back and looks down at her brother, “Daniel speak, tell them what is bothering you.” Surreal is a word to describe something that just could not nor can not be a real occurrence yet it is happening in the real of time.

This must be the time the word, surreal, was invented. The mans arm is stiff to a point that it won’t move as I try to apply the blood pressure cuff. Reaching to start the blood pressure reading I feel no pulse. “Um," I look to the nurse, “Stacy, come here for a moment please?” She turns with a look of disgust, "what now Jared can’t you even get vitals.” Refraining from commenting on her projection of ineptness I motion her to quickly come over to me. She doesn’t budge. “Ladies could you please remain here I’m going to take your brother into the trauma room so the docs can look at him right away.” They wring their hands and nod.

Reaching to touch her brother's shoulder she admonishes him. "You should speak to this kind person Daniel."

I push the wheelchair past the nurse of no brains into the trauma room. The docs come in x-ray follows. They look at me and wait for report. "This guy is dead." Thinking it is a joke they just laugh, Dr Halloren, a very kind, young blonde curly haired lady smiles and asks again. "Whats wrong with him?" She looks at him sitting in the wheel chair. He sure doesn't look well that's for sure. "It seems he lives with his sisters, they say he hasn't eaten or talked in days, rigor has already set in, feel for a pulse." stepping back I watch. Dr Halloren grab his wrist but it is stiff and yes, no pulse. Because he has been dead, for it seems, at least a few days they don't throw him on the stretcher to try to bring him back. He is so gone that he has aged already some on the other side of life. "I will talk with the family." Uma comes in to see the dead guy in chair. "I vill need help Jared."

"I will get someone to help you Uma calm down."

I walk out with the doc leaving her alone with the 'stiff.' He will be a difficult one to bag. He is stuck in a bent sitting in chair position.

The nurse looks up to see a doctor walking in and straightens her scrubs. “I sent Jared in immediately I knew he was very ill.

Dr Halloren ignores the new nurse and walks to the elderly sisters. The doc and the sisters walk out toward one of the private waiting rooms to give them the bad news.

As I sit in the chair back at the triage desk I inform the nurse. “The guy is dead and has been for a few days, I tried to get you to come over and look at him.” She sits quickly turning away from me. “How was I to know,” acting as if she is looking for something on the computer she tries to hide her embarrassment.

“We have a gunshot to the belly!” The adrenalin hits as I run to get a wheelchair so that the man carrying his friend into the triage area can plop him into the chair. I see his bullet hole, small just bellow the navel. Not a good place to get shot. He his quickly dropped into the wheel chair and away I run with one of the nurses into the trauma room. The docs do their thing and run over to the stretcher. I walk back out to triage where I belong. With a fresh adrenalin rush, something that has not happened in a long time, adrenalin rush at the hospital I am too used to working in.

Another comes in with some issues of the mind. She is a self mutilator, yet this time she had decided to put glass up where the sun don't shine. She told me it was to ease another pain she was having, that it takes away a more severe feeling. She was a frustrated and lost soul, ended up pulling out her IV and just staring ahead. she had cuts all over her arms. Self mutilation is a real illness.

One man I triaged had cut himself in the abdomen, huge slices out of his gut. I asked why he did it.. he was a nurse at one time, he just casually stated. It's an illness one just does it. As casual as that he spoke of taking a knife to his stomach to just slice across. Said it relieved him of other stuff then he just shrugged.

Biggest Loss::::

She flew through the security check. This lady out of breath and hysterical. "What is wrong? Are you able to breathe ok?" She calms herself as the words of reality now find me. "The police said my daughter has been hit by a car." "How old is she?" I ask knowing this isn't good. The woman replies with an age of young. "We don't get children here but I will check the Children's hospital here ok?" She screams as she sees her sister lying on a stretcher at the nurses station behind me. "She was with her, she was with her!" A nurse from the main ER comes over to take her to her sister.

Their children were both hit by a car while they crossed the road after singing lessons at a local school. The word that one is already dead slips into my ears from EMS. The children's hospital has a Jane Doe needing identification. Pain can sometimes be felt falling off of parents of people of ...sadness. Death of two four year olds now circles the reality channel. The police take the parents of the one child to the hospital. The mother of the other child has a broken arm. The same arm that is connected to the hand that held her daughters hand as the car ripped her from safety. They were thrown into the air. Pieces of the smallness of them lie on the streets. The mother is in shock. Triage is silent. Tears are something that don't happen often with me. But I could feel their loss and the tears lived this day on my face.

"I don't understand, I don't understand, I am so sorry sweetie oh my God!" The shriek of pain in voice to fill me when silence holds my nights. I begin to triage the next patient. Eyes do find a way to throw storms of water down your face without control of your naked thought. I cry. The patient is silent while I get her vitals. Turning my head to knock the feel of that damned fresh ripping pain of loss I see now the father running toward my triage window.

My wish for this moment...could time please do a thing of backward and remove the vehicle that hit the angels of slow and happy? He is holding his son. “My wife is here my child is here let me in!” Pushing the button the door unlocks. The father runs past me not even waiting to hear the room she is in. Suddenly through the wake of pain is the scream of anguish from the father. He falls to the floor at his wife’s bedside weeping. The ER is silent with that soft sound of tears. Yea we are human, yea we cry.

---

the rain may find its hold

and know the yellow of gold

across the dandelions breast...

but the dandelion never hides

..always open ..always wise...

soaking the rain within

dandelion dances..through time

Zombie day..:::::::

“Do you need to see someone or be seen?” The rhythm of triage is a never ending cycle of abuse illness and death. The abuse comes from the verbal onslaught from worried family members that need to see their loved one now! This is perfectly understandable but to immediately begin to curse at the poor triage tech is wrong. Triage is psychologically damaging. Some of the strongest techs have left at the end of a day of triage in tears, barely able to make it to their car without falling to the ground pounding the pavement in agony.

:::::::: love kind of sneaks up

like the bottoms of your slacks..

when you are

walking through big puddles..::

::::

Halloween was one of those days with me. An impossible 175 people triaged in one 12 hour shift was the cause of driving to the cemetery, parking the car and running wildly yelling ahhhhhh!’ The momentary loss of where the car was parked turned into the second most horrible thing that happened in the day. For this was Halloween night and the cemetery was going to close in just a few minutes leaving me trapped and away from my vehicle alone in a dark scary.... Yea bad moment. What could cause a human of intelligence to drive to a cemetery and yell? Triage, enough said.

A supposed gang member was shot and taken to the trauma room. His several thousand dollars on him were locked up. Like all valuables are done when one goes to the trauma room. The gang member's family shows up at the triage window. The concern was not for the patient but of his money. A lady of slight age holding a young child began to sway at the window staring at me. "I want the money he had on him." Well, "We cannot turn it over until and if the patient wakes and is fully aware of his decisions." Several very huge type men then appeared at the window. Looking at the bullet proof glass quickly, hoping it's intact, I then glance to the magnetic lock at the top of the door hoping it is working with full strength. Security is near but a crowd begins to form and they just sway with looks of those that could kill.

Somehow one of the big guys gets in by registration and walks up to me. "I want my brothers money dude and I want it now." Security escorts him away but he resumes his position outside the triage window.

Patients continue to sign in. They are lined out the back door of the emergency room to the street. They throw their sheets under the small window. A man yells into the intercom, “my mother was brought here by helicopter from…" They go on and on but never give a name. Always the question must be asked. “Last name please?” The phone rings with questions of nonsense. Ambulances are lining up with patients, the gangs are getting larger and there I sit, in the middle. After saying 175 times. “I’m going to get your blood pressure and your temperature.”

Construction is an ongoing beast at the hospital. One of them walked up carrying a big white board on his head. Laughing I pushed the intercom button, “dude you have to go around the other way you can’t walk through here with that stuff.” A moment of silence then the guy just smiles. “Well I would be happy to oblige, but it’s stuck to my head." Opening the door immediately after realizing this guy is a patient. I walked him into the trauma room, pushed the buzzer for all the docs and X-ray to file in. Standing for a moment I wanted to see what Dr. Johnny would do for him.

"I didn't have on my helmet at the work sight and they were throwing boards into the hole I was in. It just kind of hit and stuck." Dr. Johnny laughs a little relaxing the patient. Uma runs in, "Oh my goodness!" she exclaims then speaks some words in German. She turns to me, "how did zis happen?" I just walk out of the room to triage ignoring Uma, today I am just not in the mood for zee german girl.

As soon as I turn the corner, I hear the pounding on the bullet proof glass. Why do they pound on that damned window? Reaching to push the intercom button, I see blood all over the front of the woman that is pounding on the window. Pushing the door to unlock it I hurry her inside and take her immediately to the trauma room. She is carrying a baby, the chord is still connected to the placenta and the placenta, is falling out between her legs. Pushing the buzzer once more the many come in as I lay her on the stretcher. Stepping back to allow the docs to do their work, but the baby is not moving. There is a rush around the baby, OB comes down to assist, but it's too late. I walk out of the way, as I watched as Uma once more walk around, quickly doing nothing. She gets very frantic at times..

Triage has its rhythm's, and similar complaints sometimes come in multiples. It seems, for just a moment, that this triage day was the day to have babies in the wrong place at the wrong time.

The toilet off to the side of triage just isn't working properly, it won't flush. Maintenance is called and the plunging begins. Maintenance walks back out of the bathroom with a look of disbelief. He calls me over to the bathroom. Walking agonizingly over to the bathroom I am shown what is unbelievable. In the toilet, in the water, in the bowl is a perfectly formed fetus, still in its water home, intact but not alive is a fetus. The gel home holds this small being so neatly and comfortably, so it seems. Grabbing a basin to place the baby into, I tell the triage nurse and open the trauma doors placing the baby on a table. The charge nurses have to be called to know how to handle this. The mother is somewhere in the waiting room.

She was having pains, low pains cramping, she needed to use the restroom. She went not knowing she had passed the baby. How? Could someone pass a whole human being from their body and not know it?

I couldn't stop staring at the beauty of this small child. Not completely formed, yet curled up with thumb in mouth. Little everything surrounded by a water sac with the placenta no where to be seen.

The baby is whisked upstairs to labor and delivery and the hush is on. Have to protect the patient after all, it wasn't even born alive, or even born for that matter, but still a patient. I am pushed back out to triage, where the cavalcade continues.

"I have to get your blood pressure and temperature." As I begin to apply the blood pressure cuff, the odor of this being begins to find me. Those in life with no homes have a distinctive odor. "Why are you here today?" I ask, as I push the thermometer into the guy's mouth. With a mumble he answers, "I just don't feel good." How many times have I heard this, the very sick come to this hospital as well as the daily, nothing is really wrong types that no other hospital will take. If one is homeless, other hospitals literally tell EMS to take them to Mayville Hospital, turning the patient away from their doors. Yes, it's against the laws, but no one tells now do they.

The patient, is drunk or ETOH in hospital lingo, which means he is impaired and now known impaired cannot be allowed to leave the hospital unless someone picks him up or they rest and relax in our wonderful hospital taking up a perfectly good bed that could be for a seriously ill person. The latter usually occurs.

Back to the main this one goes, into our padded room. One of the bays in the ER has a door and has a camera mounted in the corner. Many a drunken violent type have been put into this room. One man struggling with an officer grabbed the officer's gun and began shooting in the ER. Everyone ducked, a bullet was lodged into the corner of the wall near the door. Finally subdued, the lesson learned, don't wear guns in the ER.

Another time in the room of padded for the violently drunk or combative patients an occurrence of disbelief. She is one of the wonderful caring nurses in the ER. She has the team that has the padded room. She has to get an IV into the drunk, combative patient. The patient is also spitting at anyone that comes near. A spit hood is put on over his head as they begin to try to hold him still and prevent spit to hit anyone. She begins to put the IV needle into the mans arm. He rises up quickly, catching security off guard, and bites the tip of her index finger off. She screams and stands in the main ER holding her hand up. "He just bit off my finger!" slowly falling to the floor she is quickly surrounded by staff. The patient is secluded and the nurse has to go to the hand surgeons to try to fix her finger.

Such is the life in the emergency room.

Needing a break from triage, although I have only been at triage for a few hours it has already worn me down.. Calling Uma on the hospitals communicator, it is voice activated and at first was rather a pain but now most depend on the ability to just push a button and call for, “Uma in the ER,” speak it loudly, sometimes the voice communicator is hard of hearing with the constant automated voice saying “I’m sorry I didn’t understand you.” There are two voice types one can have, female or male. I have the female voiced one, she is sexy. Sometimes I play with it asking her things to get her to say, “I’m sorry I just didn’t quite get that, can you repeat?" Sometimes when activated by pushing the button, the voice sounds low and sultry. I am on a constant to get that one. If you curse into it a male voice comes on and says “I beg your pardon.” These contraptions hang around your neck with a cloth lanyard and cause co dependence.

The german girl that gives me a moment of smile, answers in her thick german accent. “Vot do you vant?” I tell her of my need to escape triage for a moment. The trauma room tech always relieves the triage tech for bathroom breaks or those important refraining from insanity breaks. “As soon as I vinish vis ziss trauma.” Smiling I reply in kind. “Ok Uma vinish zee trauma.” ’Oh you kaluk sheizah.,” the communicator clicks off. She called me that idiot shit head name again. I think thats what it is?

Continuing my never ending flow of patient vitals one of our notorious psych patients begins to sign in. He will not stay to be seen, he just puts a few stories of random on a sheet full of stories and half truths mixed with his perspective on reality, which is a little off to the side. He will fill it out then leave, he never comes in to get his vitals, not sure why he signs the sheets, but he is a regular visitor in the triage life.

Lost...then found::::::::::

A moment of fresh life as security walks in with a small little blonde haired boy. He couldn’t be more than four years old. They found him walking the ped way near the garage. Lucky they did find him, this hospital is not in the best part of town. “What is your name?” Leaning back in my chair to enjoy the cuteness of this young one, I wait for the answer to hopefully type in the name and find where he belongs. “My name is Joshua.” “What is your last name?”

His small hands come up as his shoulders rise while his head lowers. The blonde locks curled and loose flop some as he lowers his small head. “I don’t know." How could he not know his last name? “What is your Dads name or your Moms name?” The boy turns some away from me, wanting it seems to walk back through the door where the four security guards brought him in. His index finger slips slightly into his mouth as he gestures once more. “Well..my moms name is,” there is a pause as he puts his palms up, “mom and my dad’s name is…dad.” I cannot believe how innocent this one is in spirit but still don’t understand why he doesn’t know his last name. Maybe he doesn’t know what last name means. “What is your whole long name Joshua?” “Joshua Dale Bennet.” Turning to computer I type in the name. There is a Darrell Bennet in a room on the seventh floor. “Is your dad’s name Darrell?” With a huge smile and an almost snap of a finger he says happily, “that’s my dad.” Security knows where the father is now and will escort the little one back to his parents. He walks out of triage with the four very tall security guards. Very tall to a very small four year old. He gave me a fresh of light and calm, something I needed. The fact also that he is safe and the story could have ended differently gives another good feel. “One for the good guys.”

The hours are going by, the ambulances keep coming in occupying the new nurse, while I triage, vitals only, the walk ins. They sit and watch and listen to all of the stories of the patients on the ambulance stretchers. Questions fly and they lean to hear the reply. “Do you smoke, drink, do drugs? Do you drink daily?” The patient leans a bit to see the group of people just listening to his answers and doesn’t respond. “Um.” The nurse asks again, “Do you smoke, drink, or do drugs?’ The hospital needs to know if a patient is on drugs or does them just to help in the treatment of the patient, we do not call the police if someone is under the influence of an illegal drug. The patient doesn’t answer, the nurse fills in the necessary info as much as she can, prints off the sheets and walks them back to the ER.

The time has come where the patient’s that have been waiting to be seen are showing a lack of patience. Patience, patients, similarities and the oxymoron. For a patient has not much patience, the hospital must be like a hotel to them or a place of service of all types.

She walks up, coke in hand, magazine under arm, big black purse in other hand. She is here for medicine refill, a first care patient, our place for non emergent patients. "I need to be seen, I am in so much pain, give me something for pain or a sandwich now!”

Leaning to speak into the microphone, “ma’am I have no control over when you will be seen, I will re check your vitals soon, if you could just please have a …” Interrupted quickly with spittle flying onto the window, “you, insert the Lords name in vein, piece of shit you have no compassion!” She turns and swings her purse in the air, “look at all of these people out here waiting to be seen!” “Ma’am you will have to calm down or..” She yells once more, words flattening against the bullet proof glass. I turn off the microphone so it is a little more muffled. Everyone in triage is looking at her, while security walks up behind her, waiting for the nod from me to escort her out of the hospital.

EMS brings in a screaming patient, restrained with triangle bandages, those perfect restraint devices. He begins to spit, the spit hood is immediately thrown over his head. A spit hood a marvelous invention, like a screen but instead of keeping out the flies and bugs it keeps the spit in. Sometimes the spit coats the inside of the hood, which requires an additional fresh spit hood. We can be accommodating at times. But protection is number one, and if a patient decides to throw spittle on us we must protect ourselves.

Uma comes running out, “I vill give you relief but for a zecond.”

“OK Uma, I appreciate it, danke and stuff.”

She mumbles under her breath in German and takes on the angry patient at the window. One thing about Uma, she won’t take crap from anyone. Either in English or German you will be put in your place. Uma one day had decided to curse many of the patients. She was not in a good mood. She turned to me, and looked right at me and said “mother fucker."

It seems that she had thought she was cursing in a language no one understood . "Uma you can’t curse like that at work.”

“Vot do you mean? You cannot understand me?” After informing her she was cursing in the English language and everyone speaks English, she ran away covering her mouth.

This day, though, she was cursing in German as I walked away to take my break. I understood some of the German curse words and she was tossing ‘zem’ about.

:::::

trees are quiet in their strength...

like sunlight in a dream::

::::::::

Walking through the main ER heading back to the break room I am pulled into a bay by one of the nurses, Kat, she wants me to help her hold a mans head while she puts in an NG tube. The tube of yuk that goes down your nose to your stomach, for us to either put meds in or suck things out. Kat has worked in the ER longer than anyone here. Over twenty years and counting, she knows more than the docs, but she will never say a word, unless a life is at stake. I have seen her more than once correct a resident on the wanted meds, telling of the contraindications of those meds if mixed.

And, it is impossible to hold the head of someone that doesn't want a tube stuck down their nose. This man overdosed on something and we need to fill his tum tum with charcoal, yes. The kind of stuff you grill your burgers with. It binds whatever is in your stomach not allowing your system to absorb the poisons you swallowed.

I begin my futile attempt to hold the rounded head of a human, as he starts to thrash back and forth his futile attempts are showing and spill into Kat's frustration.

"Hold his head Jared!"

Grabbing the only handles on a head, his ears, I hold the mans head in place. She puts in the NG tube and with each push as the tube moves through the patients nose down his throat she yells, "Swallow, swallow!"

Success is finally found and the tube is neatly placed in the mans stomach. Walking to finally get my break I pass a bay where they are doing conscious sedation on a patient to put a leg back into place. Another wonderful side thing of car wrecks, bones that like to push sideways or pop out of place. The docs stand on the bed, begin their contortionist maneuvers with a sheet wrapped somehow around the patient to use as a pully. The doc begins to yank and pull on the leg. The patient begins yelling in pain,

“Oh shit, ah!”

The patient screams out in pain, I cannot stop watching the procedure. The leg back where it belongs the docs are finished and they leave the room, the nurse stays to make sure the patient is stable.

“Why did he yell so much where are the pain meds?” “We gave him meds, but the medicine causes amnesia, so the person feels it but doesn’t remember the pain.”

Turning to walk out of the room

“That is just not right, no way, shape or form." The patient turns a little on the stretcher and sits up some,

“You all are good, I didn’t feel a thing.”

I just shake my head, how fair is that? You feel it, hurt like hell then forget the pain, not natural! I believe that more pain meds could have been ordered and the patient wouldn't have felt a thing. A slip of thought I assume from the doctors standpoint. Remember a patient is just a leg or a bone or a blood mass needing sutures or a rip of limb away from the body causing bothering bleeding moments. Docs get very desensitized.

The break room is just about to be reached by me but , one of the patients, an old grey haired man with a cane, is heading his way down the back hall. "Sir? You need to get back to your bed." Walking toward him to help him back to his room and in one swoosh the cane is swinging at me. Ducking quickly I say to the old feisty one, "good swing old man go on where you want to go I don't want to fight." "Damned right you don't want to fight, I want out of this place and nobody is stopping me." He turns and walks swinging his cane as he goes.

I watch one escape the ER. Finally in the break room I get a cup and a diet coke. A page overhead suddenly screams my name,

"Jared you are needed in triage!"

Uma tires of the break and is calling me back. Immediately after she pages me the Trauma page goes over the hospital intercom. It is only 11:30, seven and a half hours left of this day.

Walking back into the main ER heading back to triage, walking past the puking patients, the moaning ones in pain, the filthy ones still lying in their own blood, I try not to feel what they feel. Is it compassion or being an empath? Whatever the answer I can feel these people sometimes and it's not fun to suddenly get puky feeling or your leg begins to throb because some guy has a broken femur. Or the feeling of things crawling on you if someone comes in with lice or maggots. Well thats a normal feeling. Maybe I am 'normal'.

Triage calls

as I walk casually back to the bullet proof glass window and the line from hell.

Not in the mood for more anger, a lady walks up to the window and starts to cuss me out. Holding my hand up with my palm facing her I say

"No!"

She stops, she turns and walks away from my window. Yay!

I won that one. Suddenly, thoughts of my mother who was gravely ill in the past and subsequently died from her illness come to me. Cancer is an ugly beast that once it finds a host it doesn't leave. Chemo may stall it, radiation may slow it, but nothing kills it. Stupid infection it kills its host. A tumor decided it wanted residence behind her lower spine. Pushing it out created the look of a fin on her back. When it got to that point, she was usually not conscious either from the meds or just the fever that inhabited her along with the cancer. The body didn't want it in there and it made it very hot. She died with a temperature of 108. It could have been higher, not sure for the thermometer only went to

108 F.

A tear finds its way down my face during this rare moment of silence in triage. “Love you mom.” Knowing she is in light and love, I understand sadness, selfish for my wish to still have something to do in her life, with her life. Not my choice, mine is to follow, live and perform. Perform, that word jolts me back to physical as I see myself with the women I have had in my life.. Smiling broadly now I am enjoying the banter of my mind and soul, especially the visuals of my past loves against me in the raw fashion and wonderful invention of making love.

The triage nurse walks up behind me wanting to see if I am ok. I guess my silence startles her into something is wrong. I am usually the vocal one in life. “Are you ok?”

Settling back into reality I answer quickly.

“Oh yea I'm too sexy for my shirt.”

She slaps me on the back. I just nod and sit back again in my chair with my thoughts of life, thoughts of energy, thoughts of performing with the next love of my life, and that forever flash of every dead person I have ever put into a body bag. Gotta love thoughts...

EMS brings in a patient covered in blood. Walking over I can see the knife moving, throbbing or more like bobbing with every heart beat.. The trauma buzzer pushed they rush him into the trauma room...it seems he overdosed and stabbed himself in the heart.

I follow them to watch the flurry of doctors and the amazement of them...their eyes on the knife ...blood falls out of the wound as the knife moves with every heartbeat, up and down...drugs are pushed but he is gone. A simple kitchen knife thrust into his own heart.

The docs are fascinated. Finally the heart ceases its pump, it's want to push blood through the body. They call the time of death. The rails are down on the stretcher...that always bothers me. It must be my OCD moment in the medical world. For some reason I always think the dead will fall off somehow, as the doctor leans over to look at the knife. I pull the stretchers rail up slowly not knowing the dead man's arm is resting across the rail as I pull it up the hand of the freshly dead man is rising up against the doc leaning over the knife. The doc feels something against him. He looks down and sees the hand rising up against his chest. He screams thinking the dead man is reaching to grab him.

Trying to control my laughter I tell him quickly I was putting up the rail.. The look on the young residents face is priceless.

Uma comes into the trauma room ready to take over and bag the freshly dead. She pushes me back to triage, "go back to triage ver you belong." She and her wonderful German accent save me from another moment of surreal as I walk back thru the trauma doors out to the triage area. Where the zoo hasn't stopped its gates opening and allowing the many kind of sick types wanting attention and needing it NOW! The line of the living dead is out the door to the street. My head drops with fatigue of soul. Grabbing the next signed sheet I say what I have to say thousands of times in one day.

"I'm going to get your blood pressure and your temperature"

:::::

:::forget your shoes! drop your frown!

smell the air after rain...

run through the puddle..splash the air..

live:::::::

:::.....

Trauma time, again

Uma walks out to me happy to be able to take over triage and turn the trauma room over to my control. She is very ready to sit and just handle taking vitals.

It’s lunch time and today lunch time consists of peanut butter and crackers. I didn’t bring any lunch, so be it. Kathy the chaplain, walks past me. She tells me her wish of good morning, it is one that is the truest ever given by anyone. Never have I met anyone as wonderful in spirit as this lady is. She is a walking angel. The pain she takes on from the sorrow of the family members is beyond my understanding. But I am starting to understand taking on pain from the physical attacks of metal against flesh in car accidents or the motorcycle that flies into the ground, grinding flesh as if it is a lover.

Sitting now with my peanut butter and crackers, Kathy stays awhile to talk. She is always available to listen to anyone, and with a wisp of a thought she sends light into those that are in pain. “Jared you ok?” I sit up to look at her as she stands, her diet coke in hand, but her shoulders low and her body tired, holding too much pain on this day and it shows, at least to me.

“I seem to be getting that question a lot today,” I hesitate, should I tell her of the way I think I have helped heal others or will she think him insane. And yet with the same thought I know that she has healed many spiritually and physically.

“I’m wonderful Kathy thanks for asking.” Deciding not to burden her with his way of mind and soul I give her a break from helping others for a moment including myself. The trauma buzzer sounds once more, she heads out of the lounge to see what family she will have to talk with, I stay to eat my crackers, Uma is watching the trauma room so I can be at lunch.

Images..

Thirty minutes for lunch in a twelve hour day. Another trauma is called enough of peanut butter and crackers. I toss my cup into the garbage can, running quickly down the hall. Seven hours to go. Uma is busy tagging the patient with their temporary ID’s for trauma’s. She is happy to see me. “You vinally back vrom lunch?” Smiling I respond, “Vinally,” using my best German accent, “go to triage Uma, they await you.”

I cut off the patients clothes, all but those around the left arm. The man began his day and while using an augur, the augur won. Catching his shirt, it pulled him into its metal twist and captured his arm. His arm is twisted, pulled wrapped around the pipe. The workers on sight where it happened cut the pipe to the augur off, so it could go with the patient. It will have to be removed in surgery. The man is calm for what has happened to him, maybe in shock. I feel his silent strength and calmness. It is a comfort to me, it falls into me. I can only remove so much clothing, removing what I can for the docs to see if there is any other damage on his body. They swiftly move him to the OR, not even allowing all of the regular trauma room duties to be finished.

:::::::

petals of a flower.. silk from cottons

weave.. all wrapped up ..inside a blue

sky...   never leaving me..

;;;::::

Immediately another trauma rolls into the room. An explosion from a meth lab. Have to love the people that have ruined our easy access to the good kind of Sudafed. She is badly burned as is her partner now put in the other bay. I tag them both with the trauma tags and begin to remove her jewelry, her ring begins to slip off as I pull harder I get more than the ring. Taking rings off of people is a skill and a gift. A little lubricant just behind the ring and twist while pulling it off. The pulling hard is the key while continuing to twist. With one pull and two twists the ring comes off of this particular patient. Interesting feel as one holds a ring that is still connected to a finger and that finger is now in my hand. I still for a second and whisper,

"Oops."

Her hand is badly burned already damaged beyond, it would have come off anyway, but I didn't expect it. A sudden rush shoots through me and awkwardness begins to find a home in my thoughts. What to do with a finger and a ring? I slip the ring off and place it in the little bio bag, where the valuables are kept. Carefully laying the finger next to it's owner on the stretcher I walk away taking a moment to get over this surreal feeling. Once more the limits of flesh are seen, there is nothing they can do to help these people. The god's of trauma's must have heard it was burn day, for another one is on the way. Hurriedly, I finish my duties with the two Meth explosion patients as another burn comes in.

She was lighting her furnace, she was also stripping her floors in the basement. The two don't mix, the explosion was great. She came in 99 percent covered in burned skin. Not good, she was in no pain, another not good. If a patient gets burned, and it's not life threatening they will feel pain, for they haven't burned through their nerve endings. But, if you feel good, then you will die and soon. She gives us her information of who to call, she is alert and oriented. We didn't give her the chance to say goodbye to family, "we have to put a tube down your throat to help you breathe before it swells." The doc says, then begins intubation.

Turning I push away the thoughts of family that will never see her again in the way of alive. I hear what I know are her last words. A silence shoots through me like an injection into my skin, emptiness, silence. I feel her slip out of her flesh even before her heart stops. I here a whisper, or almost a whisper, or something, but it flies through me causing me to shudder. Her spirit must have moved through me, for the silence was light with a lift of peace.

The trauma doors open once more, another burn, another lady sitting up feeling no pain, another death that they will not give the patient a warning. She was painting her toe nails in front of a wood burning stove. The polish ignited her pajamas, leaving a burned imprint of them attached to her skin. I waited for the docs to tell her she would die, but they didn't. Of course not why should they. I finish quickly my duties and stock the bays of the trauma room.

Wham, the doors open again. He was on a motorcycle, he hit a truck and his motorcycle was broken in half. He is bloody, I put on my PPE's my 'omni podne ppe's', personal protective equipment. Yellow gown with clear face shield mask, completes the picture and the protection, and gloves of course. He is thrashing and wanting up. His skull is opened and bleeding profusely. He is waving his arms around and pulling at his IV. I grab his right arm and hand. Unbeknownst to me, he has an open wrist fracture. As I pull his arm and hand away, his hand almost comes off of his arm. Pushing it quickly back into place I hear and feel the familiar and hated crepitus. The sound and feel of bones against bones in an unnatural way is a horrible feel. The EMS worker is laughing at me as I grimace trying to hold this open fracture together. My pinky fingers slips into the gush of muscle and blood. Finally a med student takes over my holding of limb moment. I return to my duties far away from the crepitus. My face shield has small dots of blood on it and my gown is covered. Amazing how blood flies.

Another one down and another one immediately falls into my place of business. He is found down, assaulted to the face and a very huge gentleman. His face is bloodied and he is making no sense. His words are garbled. With suction and once more full protective gear on, we try to hold the man still so we can get his blood and get a tube into him to help him breathe.

His airway is compromised and that buys an intubation moment. But this man has no neck. There are many different sizes of necks in the world. I never knew or noticed this before my days in the medical world. The glorious c-collar must fit around your neck and under your chin. Some are short collars, some tall, some no neck. this guy is a no neck. The docs are not going to be able to do a tracheotomy on him because there are no visible ways to find where it truly is. So the nasal intubation will begin. This one the attending does, as he takes it from the resident who must have made an incorrect call on something.

It is a difficult everything with this one. The intubation gets done, and with one swift turn and churn the patient projectile vomits onto the respiratory therapist. Covering his face shield and yellow gown, down to his tennis shoes with vomit. I laugh, yea I sure did. We are all happy to be far away from the mess, but soon the odor finds us. Throwing towels over the puddles of vomit, I begin to try to get the famous rectal temperature.

Not knowing how I was even going to get near his bottom I stood for a moment pondering the possibility of them turning him for me. With that thought came an explosion of vomit my way. Arching into the air, and a good four feet away from the patients mouth I was about to get hit full force with vomit. My instinct was to duck.

But the top of my head is exposed. Stopping my instinct in mid vomit flight I looked directly at the vomit about to slam against my face shield and my yellow gown. Splash...with a quick whiff of odor, I was completely covered. Turning quickly I walked away and ripped off my gown. Tossing it in the garbage can I checked to see If I still had vomit on me. I was clean. And only because of my 'omni podne ppe's'.

Another one finished, my room clean, I'm clean and worn out. The doors open again, the buzzer sounds and all the folks that respond to the buzz walk into the trauma room. I put on my yellow gown and darth vader mask and gloves of course, ready for the next round of blood or poop or vomit to fly at me.

There is a moment of relief, as no new traumas come in. I walk to the main ER to help and walk right into a mess.

....

::::::: simply put

we dance we cry

we romance..

we fly..but we never

forget to rhyme......

....

A patient is standing on his stretcher, pulling his fresh bowel movement out of his bottom then throwing it on the walls of the ER bay. I reach for a pair of gloves and with a heavy sigh I walk into the shit room.. I get the patient from a standing position on a stretcher to a sitting position on a chair. Paging environmental services to help clean up the literal crap on the walls, I walk quickly back out of the room. A lady walks up to me with , nothing on her bottom, she stands for a moment and pees on the floor.. "ma'am you cannot do that why are you doing that?" She mumbles something and turns away from me as pee drips down her leg. Not in the mood for this I walk the other way.

Sometimes I have to give pause as I work to speak slowly to one or two. They cry from pain of life and pain of trying to leave it. One young one of blue eyes was getting ready to go through his normal rout of DT's, the withdraw from alcohol. He told me he was and tears ran down his face of youth. I said he needed to try to stop..that it would kill him. He talked of his beautiful girlfriend and how he didn't want to lose her. Of his dog, of his life, said he could do it if he just did what everyone wanted …to help him. He also said of the voices of alcohol that never leave… and his determination and the love of his family would help, only if he would lean to take ..that drink, the drink of freedom.

A drug addict came in.. had already been given some medicines to help? Not sure what they do for her, anyway, she was yelling at the nurses, calling them higher than's and accusing them of treating her like shit..etc etc.;; I walked up to her…spoke calmly and looked right into her soul. I carry no judgment of this woman nor of any that come in. I am no better than or worse. I am just another soul as they are, making their way through this life. I told her we needed to draw her blood, and she just needed to lie down and relax and let us take care of her. She yelled at the nurse once more, I listened as the nurse told her how she couldn't be let go because the hospital had given her some meds, and she needed to remain so she wouldn't fall.

I again spoke to her, stepping in front of the nurse to block her from this soul of sad. Calmed her, told her I would get her some food, we just needed some of her blood to get tests running so that we could help her… she relented. Then as four of us stood around her she softened and asked for someone to hug her. All three physically backed away from this soul. I said "hell I will hug ya." I leaned and let her cry some. Her words of how her life is so hard and the drugs are horrible and she was sorry for her actions. But that she still didn't like that nurse.

He came in having difficulty breathing, put him on some oxygen through nasal cannula and away the day went. Mr having trouble to breathe got bored. His words anyway, as we questioned him as to why there was a sudden flame around his face followed by his scream. "I was bored! I was just flickin my bick" Yes, he was on oxygen in the ER and decided to start playing with his lighter. His face now charred and his nostrils singed inside he just couldn't understand what happened. I told him that oxygen is very flammable and he finished my sentence with an, "I figured that out."

A moment of idiocy occurs as I am told by a new resident, Dr. Mass, to “get that patient up and walking he is faking.” I walk in the room to see a man lying flat on his back. He was assaulted and when he started to fall he put his arms back to catch himself. The only problem is when he caught himself before he fell, he hyper extended his shoulder blades right into his spinal cord paralyzing himself.

But Dr. Mass, didn’t even do an x-ray of his back, just his neck. I tell the patient he has to get up that the doc thinks he is faking. He tells me he cannot feel his legs, but then adds with determination, “just push my legs off of the stretcher, I will get up.” “Oh no, no, no, this is not a happening thing. No way dude, you relax I will get another doctor”.

The attending physician was outside the door, I motioned her into the room. After she assessed this patient she made me put the c-collar back on that Dr. Mass had discontinued. A c-collar keeps the neck straight to make sure you don’t sever your spinal cord. I watched the new resident, a green pea for sure, as I roll the patient so he can look and feel along his spine. But Dr. Mass is looking for some kind of trauma, or physical appearance of such on this mans back. I calmly state, “you don’t have to have visible trauma to have a back injury.”

Dr. Mass walks out, disgusted that this tech would question his diagnosis. Lazy or young, stupid or all of the above, this doc is missing some info in the noggin area. I take care of the now paraplegic, the man is a strong soul, he can feel it, I feel no sadness in this man, just strength..

Trying to slow my mind for a moment, looking at my watch I wish to be done with the day. Three more hours, I want away from the souls, the death and the reach that is now beginning to find me. The reach from the grave, or the stretcher as I now feel more souls reaching, hanging out. "I don't like death." Some how these words echo this time across the stock room. It begins as a small quiver. I notice I am shaking some, not a lot, just enough for me to notice. Almost like being too low on sugar and getting the shakes. It is the energy of them around me. It happens to me sometimes. I need a break and have to get outside. Walking quickly with my hidden shaking, I push through the doors to inhale the fresh air. I see the horizon full of clouds and beauty. The sun low, the air pulling at me to leave this place but I am stuck here, "until I'm not stuck here."

A break into a world of love

Romance Chapter::

A Story

Every day I listen to the sounds of morning that always lead into the evening darkness of silence with those whispers from the night life.

She walked into my life on a day of sun with a breeze that wouldn't slow its touch across me. She was selling fresh fruit grown from her yard. Her eyes struck me first with a brilliance of that look of beyond time. Many people in my day I have noticed the lack of in their eyes. No light only dull with a slam of boring crossing like a tic tac toe board into their minds.

But on this day of sun and breeze she came into my life. Her small frame held her with an elegance and softness. Her hair fell across her shoulders with a wild abandon although still held neatly away from her face with one pink ribbon. The sun on this day caught the blonde strands causing them to find a life that matched the brilliance in her eyes.

How could I stand next to this person from another time in life? A time of romance and beauty that was always held in respect.

"Would you like a few of my apples sir?" Now her voice circled me, flew into me knocking the air out of my lungs. She lifted an apple, bright with red and shine for me to see. I do not move very well anymore. My arms are slow with their reach. I tried to raise my left arm to quickly take the red apple from her hands. Wanting her to know that yes indeed I wanted to buy her apples. And possibly have a moment of her time for conversation so that I could selfishly enjoy her company and her beauty of soul.

She smiled and walked closer to me so that I could hold the fruit of her hard work. Suddenly she frowned and seemed worried. I didn't want this, "thank you, I will buy a dozen, but why do you frown?" I asked already knowing the answer. She looked at my deformity, my injury from a war of stupidity. Wars, a creation of proof that mankind is yet but a child playing with the gifts given by the universe. Messing up the face of life with heated pain and death.

Unable to stand with a steady strength and with my arms bent and crooked she frowned with a wish it seemed that I didn't have any pain. "What happened to you kind sir?" Her question caught me off guard for I didn't expect her to still be standing near me let alone to be asking me about myself.

She slowed for a moment then smiled. She lifted the apples into a basket. The park was full of young and old enjoying the day of perfect. She looked at the long path I was on and asked even another question. "May I help you take these to your home?" Her dress of cotton with small blue flowers flowed in the breeze. I caught a whiff of her scent. She smelled of lemons, yes I think lemons is what I inhaled.

I couldn't answer immediately as I fumbled for my money my awkwardness grew and this was not comfortable for me. Finally getting a grip on the dollars I handed them to her. I shook a little; it's what I do at times. But it passed and she lightly took the money from my hand, and touched me.

Now I have to say this. For in her touch a spasm of intense joy found flight through and into my core. I am blessed to have touched an angel. "I live not far, could you please help me that would be wonderful." We walked slowly at first and we talked of many things, the beauty of life, she fascinated me.

She grew fruit to help pay her bills and keep her small bit of land she owned. She was the same age as me but she seemed like that of youth. I knew I would never have anyone in my life to share the moments that I enjoyed. For I, you see am one of another time and place. At least that is what I have always felt. There are very few people that I enjoy for they are closed to the wonderful nature of life. And I am crippled in the form of flesh, not much looked on as anything of good.

She looked upon my small cottage near the edge of a pond. Slowed then smiled, "what a magical place this is, you live here?" She asked, I heard, but saw every subtle movement across her way of flow. For a moment I couldn't move. “Yes,” one word came from my mouth and that was it. I had found it almost impossible to speak for some reason around this woman. "Yes it is my home you can put the apples on the porch." I didn't want her to have to linger with a crooked broken man any longer than she had to bear.

She leaned to rest the apples onto my porch. I had to sit soon or I would fall. One of my spasms of shaking was going to hit and I didn't want her to see. I thanked her and tried to make her leave me but she wouldn't move.

It started and she watched. Her frown grew as she then reached once more to help me to the chair on my porch. Intensity of every wonderful feeling I have ever had rushed through me once more with just her small touch onto my arm. The spasms stopped as quickly as they started.

She talked with me on the porch for several hours. The time of night was finding us and I bid her to leave before the darkness would cover her walk back to the park and to her car. We talked of silly things of curious things we had seen and laughed so hard we cried. Never had I enjoyed a moment as much as I had enjoyed this moment. It came in the shape of a woman, with a cotton dress that had blue flowers and the smell of lemons.

I always remember and hold onto times of magic and ease into my place of soul. I have nothing to offer anyone that would hope to be my partner or wife. I cannot function in the way of normal that couples enjoy. She would never be able to be happy with me. I would surely bore her. My thoughts ran through my mind like this parallel with our conversation. I sure did jump quickly into having a life with a woman I had just met. But I am a dreamer and always will be.

She left but with a turn as she waved she smiled and said. "I will be back tomorrow we have much to talk of." I waved as I sat on my porch. My chair of whicker and old held me comfortably. I reached to eat one of the apples. Delicious....

In time she grew to be very fond of me. I was already very fond of her.

She came into my life on a day of sun and breeze. She became my sun and breeze. We walked through the days and held the nights with magic and vision and a touch. Nothing more is needed. For in our love, we had flight within and to our core with just a simple hold and cuddle or touch of hand against hand.

::::::::::::::::::

I see the ambulance pull up and walk back inside to wait in the trauma room.

The patient is wheeled in on the EMS stretcher. She is sitting straight up but breathing very lightly and her neck is very stiff. I wait to hear the report before starting to remove the necessary clothing. She was eating a pork chop and part of it got lodged in her throat. The guy she was with did the Heimlich maneuver but it didn't do the job. The doctors carefully examine her not wanting to push it down further into her throat. She is calm and sitting up very straight. She is afraid and the docs are being very careful as to how to proceed.

They begin to try to remove it then decide she needs to go to surgery instead. Each attempt at reaching with the forceps pushes it further down her throat. They don't want it lodged deeper into her esophagus or end up in her lungs. She is moved quickly up to the OR.

Dang, I love pork chops, "will have to chew those things a little slower from now on." Another bad thing about working in the

ER, you never know if the person survived. I still have the memory of the young girl with flowing long blonde hair, paralyzed for life, because her father didn't make her wear a seatbelt.

The trauma room is empty once more but for a moment, the mans hand is wrapped but blood is oozing through the gauze. One of the EMT's follows with a cooler. A cooler in a trauma room is not a sign of a party soon, or beer on ice. It's usually blood on ice or a limb. The man's hand is inside the cooler, looking a bit surreal to me I look at it in the ice then look up at the mans wrist, no hand, as they unwrap the gauze to see the damage. Tendons, blood oozing at first but now spurting. The man is calm,

Walking quickly out of the room I have had enough. But the vision now finds my soul and my damned imaginative mind finds the swirl begin. I am taken away into the blood and flow of life, the energy scattered in the hand wanting its attachment to the flesh it was accustomed to. The yell for a tech in the trauma room comes over the pager, and I snap out of this place of mystery. "Jared we need you in the trauma room now!" I walk back into the room quickly, I need to wrap up this hand and get it to the OR, I want this day to end now!

The clock on the wall begins to tic, sounds of triage now filter into the room, and I can hear the main ER noises, falling back into my reality.

But not until one more trauma flies into the room.

The man has no face, just flesh flapping across. One of the nurses throws a big bandage over the patient's face. It seems he wants to die, and decides to use a shot gun. The long and short of it he missed his brains and shot off only his face. Two flaps of flesh and nothing else, bony skull showing, brains intact, now that would suck, my first thought. Pain meds are given quickly, and the man is taken very quickly to the OR.

::::::::::::::::::::::___

I noticed how the sun fell ..

across my morning..

slowly, gently

arousing my thirst   to live....

....

I later learn they offered to replace the mans face, but asked him if he would kill himself again, or try. The man nodded his faceless head with a yes. They allowed him to die. Of course the face jokes flew through the ER, "I guess he just loss face." humor 101.

The clock on the wall finally releases me from this day. Dropping off my trauma shears once more I smile, but suddenly a soul filters into the locker room. “Go that way.” I point and the soul leaves me alone.

::::::::::::::::::::::::A mess another day

Cleaning the rooms is one of the tech’s jobs. And today I see Beth, a very attractive blonde nurse wiping down a bed. I do not like her doing my job. She doesn’t have to, its tech work and she is a nurse. Walking into the room I grab from her the washcloth she is using, “You are not allowed to wipe down beds, it is not your scope of skill.” She is rattled a little and leaves. Miscommunication is my main theme in life. She did not like nor understand my motives. I find out later she started a ‘get Jared fired’ campaign. But too many like me and then she began to like me. Another nurse conquered, another misunderstanding squelched.

The ER is a mess. The aroma of rotted flesh finds me as soon as I turn the corner into the main ER. Covering my nose quickly, me and odors do not get along. I see where the stench is coming from. Not a torn body from an accident but a sweet, small frail older woman. Lying in her stretcher curled up in a ball. She has all of the central lines the IV's everything needed when people just are not doing well and fluids and meds need to be put in immediately into their system.

Sharon one of the night techs sees me standing near the bay where the patient is. Sharon is in nursing school, her dark brown hair is soft as is her soul. Soft brown eyes match the package. She cares genuinely for the people in the ER. "She was found down in a cold apartment on straw, straw that was on a concrete floor." I can see the image of her now clearly as if I am there standing next to her. I can hear the whimpers of her cry and feel the pain into her bones.

Sharon tells me of how an anonymous call came in to EMS. They had to pry her from the floor. Her legs atrophied due to not moving. Her legs are drawn up to her chest, nothing but bones showing on this fragile lady. The odor is from her flesh that has rotted and broken down from the pressure of the concrete against. The skin loses blood flow quickly. When an arm falls asleep that's the first of the lack of flow. If not restored soon the cells begin to die. The skin dies then the rot begins.

:::

waters know the flow..

cool and up ..down to go..

falling I become

waters

::::

Sharon steps away quickly as the family approaches the bed. I immediately feel their darkness inside to a point of it almost blocking out their physical beings. I can see huge black swirls within them. They are nicely dressed, very nicely in fact one has a Rolex on his wrist. A lady reaches with faked compassion to touch her mother's head and seemingly brush the hair away with love.

I turn quickly also and away from the scene of false and darkness. Some of the energy tries to push into my mind but with a mere calm thought of it to be gone it flies back to its odor. The odor of souls rotted like the flesh on that victim. Choices they have and had. They chose to do this to her. I see all life as a whole of one, one light, one piece. But there is another chunk of one. That is the dark side of life. Like in the space movie, not so corny the dark side of the force does exist.

I turn to look at her once more. Without a wish to feel it, I feel her every pain. I can see her fear. The fear stabs me like several spears being shot at me in a spiritual realm. “No,” calmly spoken and slowly the spears stop their push. Choices are made and this lady is to suffer it was her choice long before she came to this physical place of existence, as is the choice of those that gave her the suffering.

I have to walk away from her it is not in my hands. I know that nothing I do when helping others is in my hands. I open to do and give whatever the one of life and creation wishes me to do. ‘I am but a servant and gladly one.’

I have fallen deep into thought of life and consequences. The reality that we all still have choices in this life. We can choose the dark of energy or the light of energy. One has a consequence of the rhythm or the flow of that level of vibrations. Juan slaps me on the back snapping me out of thought. “Dammit Juan don’t do that man!” Juan laughs and steps back,.

Juan is happy but turns back to the ER. Seeing the chaos he groans, "Is it time to go home yet?” His watch says no it its digital facial expression. “Yes for me it is!” Turning away from Juan I leave him to the ER mess of the night.

‘Transaction accepted’ the computerized voice allows me to leave once more, good ole gatekeeper.

Turning back to the main ER Juan is also ready and wishing he could go home. But his shift is far from over. Another psych patient is brought in. The obscenities fly against anyone and everyone near. The nurse at triage tries to ask this person that is lost inside his own mind. “Do you drink smoke or do drugs? Do you want to hurt yourself or others?” “Yes I want to hurt you and every person in here." Security is close as are the police officers. The shroud of control is still in place false in its way of walk for no one is ever safe, especially at this ER.

“””””””””””””””””””””””’

Looking down at my boots thoughts fly like dust on a windy day across and through me. I feel totally alone and the silence that finds my core is not one I am enjoying. “I have always been alone why is this different?” The van welcomes me with a cold feel. Sitting, I look once more at the stars through a dirty windshield. Watching my hand grip the steering wheel I wish there was a she, waiting for me. Looking toward the passenger side of my van I see an imaginary love. Her smile warming my.. memory of what possibly could be in my future? My thoughts are being stupid tonight.

Keys turning in the ignition I see this imaginary love crossing her legs to tease me while out at dinner. Or the way she leans over the table to serve me a drink, knowing I am exploring her every inch. "Ah love, will it ever return to me?" Looking straight ahead I drive slowly into the darkest night I have ever felt.

Now the crawl begins, it is a slow crawl of darkness. The sound is of a something not of this world. Not of the world of those with eyes that only see the one level of life. Negative energy lives and thrives and demands to take over anyone that is weak enough to allow its filter inside. The choice always the holders, but what can one do when choice becomes invisible. They have been labeled emotions and 'normal'. In reality they are the swirl of darkness that robs so many of their light, of their forever that is waiting to be lived. Hiding behind fear, lust, envy, jealousy zapping into the core of the ones of weak and familiar complacency.

Circles of the many women I have had in my past flip through the pages of my thoughts. Lust is a consuming beast, phone sex, live sex, any sex. I was trying to fill an empty spot. Trying to find love, trying to prove myself as a real man. Able to take any woman I was with to a place higher than she had ever experienced in the sexual field. But it left me emptier with each stroke of flesh. Finally deciding to stop, I refused to play the game any longer. Now I wait for that elusive angel called love.

Not sure it will exist in my future, but very sure I have tasted ever facet of sensuality looking for it.

My apartment is ready for me to fall into the wonderful purple bath. Lavender aromatherapy is a heaven and a wuss factor that can never be told to anyone. My secret of relaxing is my purple baths. Slipping under the water silence is found, finally. Meditation is an interesting place, teasing the soul to walk while thoughts through the brain are shut down. Always reaching to know the why's of life I meditate. But the universe is slow in explaining my why's in life. So I keep walking like zombie dude, ..teasing my mind with images of love.. flexing my muscles with that physical lift..always wanting.. always seeking a normal flow.

Always needed::::::::::

The hospital is alive with patients that are not all surviving. Every room doubled and not enough staff leaves the patients not cared for and the staff on duty exhausted. Donna is charge nurse on this day from normal chaos. She begins to call people in to work. I am off this day but on the top of the list of techs. The phone rings she waits. Donna is a slight of build lady with a feisty energy. She is a good nurse with frustrations on how the ER is run, just like most that work in the world of medical. It seems time has shown that more and more people are falling ill and more and more are visiting Mayvilles ER.

She gives up quickly on me and calls Vera, then Brian. No one is answering. Thinking for a moment she pushes the numbers that will cloak her phone number. That way they won't know she is calling from work. It works. I answer with a voice of slumber and comfy. "Jared this is Donna we need you can you help today? Maybe work a few hours please please?"

I sit up in my bed seeing that I still have on my clothes. "Jared just nod yes and get in here as soon as you can I will be waiting for you." She hangs up not giving me the option to reply. Although she has no right or way to make me come in she knows I will. I am the fool that will always work when asked, even at the expense of myself.

Vera is another one that comes in, in a heartbeat always taking advantage of the overtime pay. She also works very hard and I am very fond of her. She is a beautiful lady of much intelligence and humor.

Donna calls others to come to work, as she is on the phone while it rings a drunk patient in the holding room is screaming how he wants to kill everyone in the place. On the other end of the spectrum there are several cries of pain. A patient in bed one that is near where Donna is on the phone, is getting her shoulder put back in place. The patient in the very next bay is getting the luxury of a pin being screwed through the skin between the bones to hold traction on a fracture in the leg. Some how magically no one ever has enough pain meds. Heaven forbid a patient shouldn't hurt.

Uma is staying on for a few hours. She has been working the night shift and is still wide awake. There are at times some speculation as to whether she takes drugs or drinks on the job. Something has to account for her behavior of try to kill zee patients. "Uma thank you for staying a few more hours this morning." Donna speaks quickly to her then walks over to the drunk patient.

The drunk is a full foot taller than she is, but she puts him in his place. "Sir you have no right to talk to us that way now just go back in the room and be quiet until you are sober." She points to the padded room. He turns with a grunt and mumbles some obscenities. Uma walks up to her. "Vou are so brave to do zis thing vou do." Uma smiles and pats her lightly on the back. "Well thank you Uma." Just as suddenly as he gets quiet, he blows up once more. This time spitting his way into a spit hood given quickly by security. Uma runs away not wanting any part of 'zis man'.

~~~~~~

~~~~~~~~~~~~~~~~~~~~~~~~~~~~~~~~~~

The drive to the hospital is fast. Walking through the main ER I wish once more I had stayed home.

Moaning loudly I slam my fist into the back hall wall.. A patient across from the hall laughs. "Having a bad day?" An elderly lady sits on the edge of her stretcher. She wants to go home. Turning I smile at her. "What is the saying? Women can't live with them can't live without them." She smiles then asks to go home. "Why are you here? What is wrong?" She moves with animation and a bit of cuteness. Her white hair wrapped up in a bun on the top of her head but its a mess up there. She must be a psych patient for she doesn't seem to be ill of flesh.

::::::::::

toes in the sand...command

attention to detail.. every grain examined

with a smile of abandon...

::::::::

The patient sees the frown on my face and laughs. “You want to go home too I see.” I listen to the rest of her story. It seems she was picked up from her home. Someone called EMS on her because she was drunk in her own home. This is just wrong. She is quite intelligent and is a professor at the college. Yet because she has a drinking problem, which she admits to, she is reported as not safe and hauled to the hospital. The shift as of late in the world is with the taking away of rights. It is insidious and people do not see it. They nod along doing their normal day. “Why is the charge nurse doing this?” I say out loud with disgust as I begin to leave her on her stretcher. But the charge nurse comes in, “have to take off your clothes ma’am you are on a hold because you are drunk. The old lady shifts and then states, “No,” as her reply. I nod along with this. “She hasn’t done anything..." The charge nurse shoots a look at me, shutting me up pronto. She leaves me to the task of removing the drunken ladies clothes.

After a battle of wits and conversation I remove the clothes of the old lady. She is allowed to keep on her underpants but that is it. As I begin to take her jeans off she just lays back and spreads her legs. Her very, very, dry legs. The dry skin flakes off as a dust cloud forms near my face. Security has been there to help with the removal of clothing. They suddenly step back away from the woman and outside of the bay. Leaving me stuck in the fresh skin cloud.

Learning to not breathe temporarily in the emergency room is a gift. One never knows the odors that will find your nostrils. Immediately I cease my breathing. Hurrying to bag her clothes and get out of the room. Taking a gasp of air as I leave the room, security just laughs at me.

A prisoner startles me as he walks past on crutches. He seems to be moving pretty quickly and the crutches are ill fitted. I began looking around wondering where the guard is that belongs with this prisoner. The sounds of chains clashing somewhere in the background, reminds me immediately of that Christmas movie and the spirit with the shackles. The lost guard approaches juggling the shackles that should have been on the prisoner. Instead of putting them on, he is walking, running to catch up to him carrying them. “Whoa dude those crutches aren’t fitted right to you.” The prisoner seems nervous but I don’t pick up on it. But instead of fixing the crutches I decide to let him move on down the pike. One of my peers fitted him to these crutches who am I to stop him. He moves quickly once more away from the guard and out of the ER.

After putting the ladies clothes in the locked closet I walk over to talk with the secretaries to kill some time. Katie and Liz are working this day. Two of my favorite 'sexytaries' a nickname I uses for secretaries. They are usually sexy and all made up beautifully to present to the world their skill in typing arranging and being sexytaries, I usually confuse their names though usually calling Katie Liz and Liz, Katie. They are used to it. Katie a young twenty two year old doing the necessaries to get into medical school, is quick with wit and very beautiful, for a kid. Liz also young with those eyes of pure light always gives me a smile. She wants to be a tech in the ER but because she is such a great secretary they won't let her. She also is in school for the doctor lands.

"Any cool phone calls today?"

Leaning now against the counter I await a story from the lands of odd.

"A lady called in saying that we took her ability to do her wifely duties, because of the irritation due to a catheter we put in".

Liz just laughs then makes one of those expressions she is known for. Her face can move in an instant showing her immediate thoughts at the moment. She is a cute little one with short dark hair and brown eyes. "You could never play poker Liz" Liz retorts quickly with a "I play Texas Holdem all the time and I do well I might add" I nod, "then consider me wrong." Katie slams the phone down quickly. "I was just assaulted on the phone."

I wait for the story. "Tell us the story Katie" "Some guy kept asking me for medical advice, I said we cannot give out medical advice over the phone if you feel you need to come in then do so."

"And?" "He begins to tell me he has puss on his dick and could I suck it off for him." She picks the phone up once more and slams it down. "Tada, I was assaulted!" "You should have hung up quicker" Liz laughs as another phone call comes to mind. "A lady called yesterday saying her bowels were falling out and what should she do?" "What did you tell her?" "The standard cannot give out medical information. The caller replies with "It's the end of the world, the bible says and the bowels will fall!" I hung up quickly."

The television is on with a breaking story. It seems a prisoner that was a patient in the ER from Maysville has beaten his guard with a traction weight and took his gun. He is now holding hostages. "So that's why the guy was so nervous." Realizing the prisoner that I stopped momentarily to adjust his crutches was hiding one of those traction weights as he ran from the guard. I am thankful I didn't do anything or I could have been the one that was beaten.

As I finish cleaning one of the rooms a patient is brought in. A prisoner has cut off the tip of his finger some how. The bright orange one piece outfits the prisoners wear do stand out. Usually they are shackled as this one is. I care not why they are walking in chains, none of my business I treat them still as humans needing help in the ER. The finger tip is put in a specimen cup and placed on the counter outside the bay near the secretaries. Moving him quickly into the room I prepare the patient to go to the OR.

But something is missing and no one knows yet. Not noticing the clank clank sound what is thought of as a child's toy. The prisoner heads up to the OR for them to attach his finger. As I roll him into the pre op bay they ask for the finger. I look under the stretcher and even feel in my pockets. "I don't have it do you have it?" Hurrying down to the ER I ask if anyone has seen it. But it has mysteriously vanished. So no attachment will occur but they do sew up the end of his finger. Katie stops for a moment as she begins to laugh uncontrollably. "There was a kid here walking back and forth with something in his hand shaking it." The clank clank of the toy was the prisoners finger. "Well I guess he can put his finger on it then huh?" Obviously the kid left the ER with the finger tip.

"Uma?" She stops for a moment and turns to me looking very confused. "Jess?" which I assume means yes, "what are you carrying?" "Zis looks like a leg, I found it on the floor near zee patient but zay say it isn't zairs? I just don't know vut to do Jared." Two bays down from the room she found the leg is a man that is frantically looking for something. He is hopping around with much energy. "Uma look, it is his, take it to him." "Oh my goodness I veel so dirty." She walks quickly to him, he is happy, she is relieved. Quickly washing her hands she makes an ugly face. I smile at her what a trip she is.

One of the patients from the wonderful padded room has found a way to escape. She has also escaped from her hospital gown. Flying past me with a look of glee and giggling, she is naked as a jay bird in flight. Uma runs after her with a sheet hoping to catch her and cover her. "Stop! Stop! Vou must stop, vou cannot do zis!" She is making a lap around the full ER. The visitors and the patients get a laugh out of this. "This is a good thing," the whole ER is laughing as she runs past each bay finally coming to rest on the hip of the large and in charge nurse, David. He is a big man that is a plus to have around. He usually helps handle all of the violent situations in the emergency room. This time he tackles the naked giggling jay bird. Falling to the floor he pulls her down but she ends up on top of him. Uma catches up to them and throws the sheet quickly over her. Flying past her it covers nothing of her, but totally covers David's head. "Oh my goodness zis is not right!" David shifts his weight causing her to fall to the floor. The sheet lifted and wrapped around her quickly. The scene slows to an end. The ER is erupting in laughter.

~~~~~~

Kim is another fun nurse at the ER calls me over to help her with a combative patient. She has long dark hair that she wears back in a pony tail. And a humor that I enjoy and she has also done a rare thing. She has given birth to five children.

"Help me Jared!" The patient is an older woman with eyes of wild and crazy. She is obviously out of her noggin either on drugs or just mentally not right. Kim has to put an IV into this wild one to give her some meds. "Calm down, you are in the hospital we are trying to help you." Holding down her left arm with my right hand and her leg with his my left hand I think I have this side of her under control.

Uma runs in to help and holds the other side. Suddenly the feel of fingers of steel begin to rip into my right butt cheek. Yelling out
~~~~~~

with a "Youch!" moving my hips quickly to the left away from the patient's grasp I start to laugh. "She just tried to rip most of my bottom off." Uma is laughing so hard she lets go of her arm. Kim is now on the receiving end of a right cross that floats across and catches me square on the jaw. Falling back some I can't help but laugh. Kim joins the group in laughter as the patient just squirms and sits up, then drops all the time her wild eyes seeing what she perceives as her enemies. Finally getting her under control the IV is in and away they go to another adventure in the ER. Although the violence is dangerous but difficult to stop. We try to laugh at the moments and protect ourselves at all times.

I am floating this short day at work. A float turd doesn't have a team of patients but helps with the small jobs. Stocking the bays, helping where needed. An elderly lady is lying on a stretcher as I walk past. "Hello ma'am we will get you off that hard board in a little bit." Every patient that falls anywhere will be transported by EMS via neck brace and hard back board.

She smiles at me and is very calm. "Thank you, you sure are a happy hurt person why are you here today?" She smiles even bigger. "I was playing tennis on my WII and fell into the mantel and got knocked out." "Well, our first WII injury, welcome to the hospital, we will get you taken care of and back to tennis soon."

Her energy feels good. She has lived a life full of love and giving. I see in a flash the complete of her life. She is a good one.

He is rolled into his room on a stretcher. An eye patch covers his left eye. The whispers fly when an odd trauma occurs and this is one of those odd ones. He was driving down the interstate with his wife. Just driving along minding his own business, when wham! A turkey breaks the windshield and its beak pushes into the mans left eye. He must have had some old curse that finally came true...::you will have your left eye plucked out by a turkey while you are driving, ::curse?

The very next room holds another elderly lady. "Anything I can get for you?" She smiles then starts to stand up. Grabbing the right side of her hip in pain she sits back on the stretcher. "Whoa, sit down feisty one where are you going?' She shifts a little on the hard stretcher, "I want to leave I'm ready to go I thought you were coming in with my discharge instructions."

"I will check on it." "Kim, is she ready, the lady in bed 7?" Kim still laughing at him getting goosed nods with a smile. "Do you know she is 99 years old?" "No way!" I walk quickly back into her room. Always wanting to know the whys of life. I ask my question that is always asked to the elderly patients. "What is the secret of life? Have you figured it out yet?" She smiles a little then speaks quickly on her likes.

“Well, I never drink any of that pop, that is not good for you.” I enjoy my pop I don’t like hearing this. “I walk a lot and eat red meat.” She grabs her hip again. "You don’t look comfortable, let me help you back in the stretcher.” She is no bigger than a minute. With one lift and slight pull she is sitting better in the stretcher and looking much more comfortable. “Thank you ,you are very nice.” “I will check on your papers.”

Kim is standing right behind me with her instructions. She has a broken hip, but it’s not enough of a break for her to need surgery. A broken hip and barely a complaint, a generation of strong types that doesn’t exist in this day.

Beth walks past me quickly moving toward one of her motorcycle trauma patients. He is not doing well. He is a soldier that was doing over eighty miles per hour on his bike and crashed. “How is he Beth?” Leaning on the stretcher rail I watch Beth work the meds for this patient. She is genuinely concerned and genuinely frustrated. “He is not doing and won’t do. I have to get him up to the OR immediately.” Blood from the patients left ear is pouring down onto the stretcher. A small pool is forming at the base of his head. His eyes are swollen shut and purple is now the color of his eyelids. “He is paralyzed from the neck down he has a head bleed I have no idea what they will do with him at the

OR but they want him now." I get the portable monitor to put with the patient for transport. "I will help you Beth," she continues to arrange and push meds through his IV. Shaking her head then looking back down at the syringe she pushes the meds and sighs.

A shift once more of those invisible types move around me. Ignoring them has become a work of the day. I wonder why they appear at times and at other times they are gone.

Quickly they drop the patient off at the OR. As soon as I get back to the ER I have to take another fresh dead to the morgue. Meeting security at the door I maneuver the stretcher into the small area near the cooler. As the door opens I see an autopsy is occurring. My breath stops for a moment. The chest is cracked open. The organs are being taken out, and the crowning glory is a head full of red hair. I saw this man in triage just a couple of days earlier. He walked in, not feeling right. I remember his wild red hair, it reminded me of the actor Danny Kay, his red hair long and unruly. Now his body is cracked open. "I guess he didn't feel right."

I find out that he was full of cancer. They opened him up and he died immediately. Not a bad way to go I guess, not knowing you are going to go like most other cancer victims. "Red hair..bouncing"

“”

I know I saw an angel..

the night i saw..

light with air.. peace with care..

and love surrounding my

heart::

Walking back into the ER I find several traumas occurring. Three teen age types found pushed into the back of their cars, no seat belts worn, no way to tell who the driver is. Since I am floating I help with the many trauma’s.

“I don’t feel a pulse, we need CPR now!” My hands on the chest of this seventeen year old . Pushing to pump the meds that are now being delivered through central lines. Pushing to pump the oxygen that is being given by the respiratory therapist through the bag valve mask. Pushing to do what the heart does so easily every day every second. My sweat begins to drop on the young one. “Stop compressions.” The docs look to see if there is any rhythm, if the heart is beating on its own yet. “Continue compressions.” I can feel the spirit of this man leave slowly. It is seeping out of him like a leak in a rubber boat and the air is finding escape. I push harder and faster. Suddenly two ribs break. A common occurrence while doing CPR but I keep pushing.

I hear them call the time of death of the other teenager in the other trauma bay. Pushing harder now and faster I yell "No!" to this fresh of life. But nothing is working. He is too badly broken inside he is bleeding out. He is bleeding internally everywhere and his heart has stopped. They tell me to stop compressions but I cannot. "No," I say this time in a whisper. I am gone for a moment into the feel of this young soul. I hear him cry to be still alive, just as suddenly as I hear this I hear a whisper of release me. Stopping the compressions I stand.

Sweat is falling freely, my arms are full of blood causing my muscles to swell. A silent thank you for trying some how floats into my mind with that way of voice with no voice. Suddenly, I feel the soul of the young one move across to the other bay. There is a liquid feel of peace, "he was a good kid," as they close the kids eyes. Now I have two bodies to put into bags.

Darkness moves into the room and filters around the other teenager. It seems to infiltrate him pulling on him. I push a thought of get lost, to the dark light causing it to stop and move across to him. But it doesn't mess with me. The docs snap their fingers in my face. "Bag em Jared." Everyone leaves the room after the call of death occurs. Some of the nurses stick around to do their paper work. But I am left alone with the bodies. I call for Kim to help. "I need you to turn this dead kid so I can put the body bag under him?" "Oh, just what I wanted to do today," as she rolls the body without warning the kid passes gas. I have learned to stop breathing in rooms when odors find their way, this was an immediate cessation of breath. No one wants to breathe in the fresh gas of a dead person. Quickly pushing the bag under the kid I move away gasping for air. Kim cannot stop laughing as she holds the dead boy.

Looking down at the boys face, I touch his hand and say, "rest in peace youngen and tell my mom.. hello." Putting a sheet over the body bag I begin to cover the evidence. Family is ok with seeing comfy blankets and soft white sheets but not the plastic of a white body bag covering their loved ones face.

written because of the loss of lives....................

Seat belts

For the past 36 years I have driven a vehicle of some sort. The past laws did not include nor stress wearing a seatbelt. Most of the cars didn’t even have belts that even worked back in the day of my youth. I am one of those that would say, "Me? Wear a belt? You cannot make me. I don’t need one ..etc etc.. I have been driving for how many years?" Blah, blah, blah, on and on the words go. Interestingly enough, it took a shock factor to stimulate my interest and now deepest desire to remain alive after taking a driving trip. It's called, working in the ER of a level one trauma hospital.

I have had to do the CPR compressions on the 15 year old that showed barely a mark upon his body, but inside, he was broken apart. Guess what, we can't fix that. No seatbelt worn on that day for this youngen. No, he wasn't driving. No the driver wasn't drunk.

The driver by the way died also. He was in the other bay at the ER. As I heard them call his time of death, I pushed harder on the young ones chest, hoping upon hope he would not cease to live. As I began to clean this youth and put his body, now freshly dead, in a body bag, the pain of the waste took me over. This has to stop, and if a few words on a page or my voice of past experiences of these young dead will help, then allow me to indulge you, and possibly with the luck of God, save a life.

The term 'seat belts save lives' yea, yea, we hear it all the time, but do we truly understand or even believe it? No way, for as I stated earlier, I was among the ones of yea, yea.

She was 17, and was not belted into the seat of vehicle. She will now never walk again. Ah, guess what, sometimes we don't die. Thrown from the car, she was twisted like a rag doll, spine now in two different places. If she had a seatbelt on, the damage would have been less. Possible death still? Yes. But the odds so greatly improve when wearing the belt that keeps you from being flung into the car and metal, or thrown onto the pavement.

Another life now not breathing was a 27 year old, no belts.. go figure. He was thrown from the car, head hitting the pavement twisted his head around. His body was found face down, but his head was looking straight up. Hmm, a belt of simple click.

The list of unfortunate sadness and loss could go on and on. Daily, that's every day, someone of teen age or older die because they do not wear the belts. Because the news does not show the loss we assume, yea, yea.

After trying to cover the boy's brains from easing out of his eyes so that the parents wouldn't see the ooze, the waste of life comes to mind. I worked one week and had 7 deaths of teens from lack of wearing a belt. Seven lives now that are no longer for the reason of ignorance and stubbornness.

The car will not protect you and the hospitals cannot fix you if you are broken up inside, or your spine takes a dip to the side. The body travels the speed you are driving, slamming, ripping, twisting you.

Two teens found at a scene brought to my ER. They had no idea who was driving for they were laying on each other unconscious in the back window above the seat, crammed like sardines against the broken glass. Both died. I washed one up for viewing. His hand had a small cut and as I washed the blood away, I looked at the face of this boy. Such the innocent, and young, and .. dead.

A mother still lying on the backboard in the hospital bay is told her daughter didn't survive the wreck, seat belts not worn. There will be some punishment for her along with now the loss of her own daughter. It was just an accident, but she is now gone.

Drive as if your life is about to cease. Slowly move through the traffic. Wear your seatbelts. Trust me, the brains do ooze from your ears and your eyes and your nose, and there is nothing that can fix it. A simple CLICK of the belt and the realization that you are human and fragile will save your life and your friends that ride with you.

Driving with the booze::

Real short statement here…. I also have driven in my past youth, while I was under the influence. Thank God, I didn't kill anyone or myself. No, I do not do it anymore. Designated drivers save lives and allow you to have that glorious hangover.

The father came into the trauma room, drunk, laughing, asking about his kid that was riding with him. Well, the kid is now dead for what reason? Driving drunk and no seatbelts. The father will now served time in prison and the son will never breathe again.

The youngen was awaking from his drunk stupor. He asked of his friends that were in the car with him. As the officer stood outside the bay, I saw him lean to tell him the news. His friends were dead. And this young one of 19, that went out to just 'have some fun', has now killed his friends and will serve many years of his life behind bars.

Yes, driving drunk kills. Yes, get a designated driver. Yes, you will be punished to the extent of the law if you kill someone while driving drunk. Yes, it is worth the trouble to save a life, your own, or the other, and to keep yourself from being behind bars.

Yea, yea you say.. it won't happen to me. I will remember that as I zip the bag up over your head and wish you to find peace.

::

The day is filling with sunlight. Warmth follows the sun and the play in life begins. Job security for hospitals, people don't play safely. I want to be out in the sun and away from this old visitor. A gift they say more like the curse they also say. When a body of life is given vision to see the altered reality in life called the lands of spiritual, the plank of normal walk is removed leaving the one of 'gift' alone with only their faith.

A shrill scream from the main emergency room creates a visual of a haunted house. Walking back into the mess of bodies all screaming. Another contrasting moment is the feel of anger from a restrained patient lying on a stretcher in a room as I walk past. Balance in life. She is restrained and talking with slurred speech. Needing help so she 'screeches'. I lean into the room "What do you need ma'am?" She looks to see who is walking into the room.

Lying flat on her back legs stuck open from the leather restraints on her ankles she is in very much a vulnerable state. Her hands equally bound by the restraints completes the picture of a normal out of their head patient in the ER. One cannot walk around half naked in the emergency room. If one does one will be tied down to bed. "Come here I can't see you." She says with a slur to me. Leaning over her to let her see my smiling face. "Why don't you feel my titties while you are in here?'" Her eyes are glassed over but the point is made. "I don't think so ma'am that's not in my scope of skill as a tech." I get out of there quickly, not wanting to be accused of accosting her. Her nurse is Justin.

Now, Justin is one of high morals and just a plain ole good guy. I pat him on the back as he walks past heading into the room with the wild lady. "Be careful in there," Justin smiles, "hey Jared?" Pausing as he finishes mixing some meds for the patient he looks at me. "Be careful with these meds? Oh heck I know what I am doing." He walks into the room. I wait. Looking at my watch, just a few seconds goes by before Justin walks quickly back out of the room. "Told you to be careful in there." Justin looks a little bit pale, "You ok?" "I just vomited in my mouth, she asked me to do some pretty nasty sexual things to her. I will never be the same." I just smile at Justin, "You will forget it soon," passing my hand over Justin's head acting as if I am doing the Jedi thing, causing his mind to forget what just happened. With a zombie walk away from me, he nods and repeats in a monotone voice. "I will forget it soon."

"I can lift my legs for you," the patient of large says quietly as I walk into her room. She needs to be cleaned and has requested her tech to do this duty of non pleasure. She comes to get touched, not to get treated. I begin to refuse doing this chore just as a new tech walks up "I will help you Jared." I step to the side not wanting the soon to inhale odor of lost lands and closed legs. She says quickly as the wash rag approaches her, "I can lift my legs for you," with one quick movement, she moves like a contortionist. Her legs literally beside her head, exposing what is the most expansive amount of flesh with odor, I have ever witnessed or had the honor to smell. I begin not to breathe and watch the slow motion of the other tech wiping this patient of weird. “You are very flexible,” I state flatly trying not to gag. Her mass of bottom is at least a foot long from top to bottom.

It is not the size that is disgusting, it is her legs planted neatly at her side with that look of glee on her face, that is disgusting. She lowers her legs with the same speed she lifted them as the other tech stops cleaning, saying she is finished. I cannot wait to leave this room. The doc stops my motion of walking away as she walks up. “Jared assist me with this pelvic exam.” I contort my face with the loudest silent look I can conjure but it didn’t work. “Certainly,” I say with monotone and no enthusiasm.

I step to the side of the patient. I wait for the words. The doc informs the patient of need for pelvic because of her reasons for being at the ER. The patient smiles as the doctor begins to lean to get into position to slip the speculum into this ladies vagina. “I can lift my legs for you.” Swoosh, with one swift movement of an acrobat, the legs rise and stay in their place of trained. The doc just says “ well well,” as the speculum goes in, the doc visibly gags.

Ending the exam quickly she leaves the bay. I leave the bay. WE leave the bay. I am traumatized for life now. This is the absolute worst visual in my whole entire medical life. I may never want to touch a woman again. Smiling at that thought I say out loud, "nah". The day continues as I beg the doctor to discharge her. A bad moment that will take twenty thousand years to remove from my mind.

Patients have at times accused nurses and docs of doing some nasty things to them. It's usually a good thing to have someone come into the room with you with those types as a witness. But sometimes an accident occurs and something may be construed as a sexual act. A medical student is struggling on this day with his procedures needing to get done. The residents make the medical students do the grunt work for them. Things like pelvic exams or butt exams for that wonderful search to see if you have blood in your rectum. If one comes in with abdomen pain we have to check the bottom.

The medical student arrives on the scene. A few minutes later a very red faced medical student walks past me out of the room. Looking into the room I see Kim laughing that silent laugh. Her shoulders or moving but no sound is coming out, "what Kim?'

The patient is also laughing. When doing the exam, the medical student turned the patient on her side and proceeded to insert his finger into the wrong opening. As he probes she quietly states, “you are in the wrong hole.” He says his apologies puts on new gloves and finishes the rectal walking out quickly. Hence the red face. The patient yells, ‘Woohoo, I haven’t had sex in three months I’m going to tell all of my friends to come to Mayville’s emergency room!’ Shaking my head away from this thought I leave the room. “Whew.”

After the patient is discharged the staff begins the humor. “We will have doctor long finger see you next time.” On and on it goes as the light of a bit of slip of hand and slip of finger finds laughter in a place of usual sadness.

::::

peek a boo..

a time or two... smiling as the wind

blows... tossing me a

rose..

:::

The flight of duty the way of need finds me once more as I have to help with a procedure, holding someone's leg so that the ortho people can put a screw through it to hold it in traction is not bad.. It's on the "kind of cool," factor. But holding an obese man with legs three feet wide so the nurse can locate his very small unit is not fun. This day finds me holding with much effort a thigh that is as big as my torso, watching as the nurse reaches to find the smallest piece of equipment I have ever seen. The body shouldn't, by the laws of life be allowed to grow as much as it can. Why does nature do this to human kind? I cannot figure out the reason for obesity. To cause people to be trapped in these huge vessels. Why? Is it a punishment from past lives? The 'unit' is found and the catheter is inserted with a result of wonderful urine. Walking quickly out of the room I have no judgment on this one of large, just compassion.

The gloves come off my hands quickly as I snap them from a distance into a garbage can. "Two points." One of the newer chaplains comes up behind me pressing herself against me. The feel of her breast is very obvious as my arm is now the object of her affection. "Well hello Diane and how is your day?" She continues to hold my arm against her breast. Walking quickly away from her I have no idea what that is about.

Circles are continual; they surround and grow but are always circular. Memories find the past and the dance of tests. When one is enlightened and eyes are opened to the supernatural. Faith has to be, and will be tested. Will you still remain humble? After you heal a person will you remain humble? After you see into the future will you still hold onto the light in life, or gather the darkness of negative around you to use at your bidding. For they wait for you to call on them, for therein lies the rub.

The power and the knowledge of power on earth given to the one if just a whisper to the way of dark finds it's mark, then that place of tease begins. Difficult to let go of power, that power to hurt someone if they mess with you, by sending a thought to the ones of dark to flip the motorcycle they are riding or to cause their bike to mysteriously get hit by a car. Yea, it's real but so is the light. And sometimes just sometimes, people will be protected by the universe. The mark against the soul will be on the user of the bad guys energy.

::::::::::::::::A moment of thought:::

Borrowed

This breath of air we so easily pull inward without pleasure of giving back the wish of thank you. Clothes are borrowed as well, the books upon the shelf, the car we drive..all borrowed. Is it too fresh to say we borrow this birth of life also? Of course not, we know we are mortal and our flesh so easily ages with time of smiles and frowns, ups and downs, etc...

Why do I trample among the leaves, pushing a foot into the reality that they were borrowed by the tree? Now we see the beauty of colors and gasp, oh so wonderful this plethora of colors and shapes. But we witness the end of a life, albeit, not of the flesh that we are accustomed to, but life nonetheless.

So, do we find that life when ending its borrowed function, has a beauty unlike its lifetime? But I have seen the end of life across the trauma table at the emergency room. And that is not a sight of beauty; it is barely something that can even be witnessed. So we find the beauty of the end of life has to be seen with different perspective.

The beauty of death from this life, is the belief that the energy, or soul that we hold within this shell, is magnificent and now set to fly into the place of real birth. Yet, the shell does not have the beauty that nature gives for our pleasure, when death occurs with humans. The opposite occurs, almost as if to show us, this is not the life that we feel to our depth, it is just fragile meat and bones. We grow accustom to the sight of eyes with soul behind, the walk of our muscles through our emotions. When the body is emptied of the energy of the stars, we turn away. Closing the shell up into a bag, or burning with flames.

Borrowed time they say, borrowed life, is what we explore. When something is used, we take it to its limit. Enjoy the flavor of the peach and the texture of the ground beneath our feet. Every item we use or supposedly own it is just that, temporary and borrowed.

What does this tell my thoughts? Borrowed, they are also, to grow into another and yet another.

To witness the change of seasons with nature is beautiful, even with the tree's trunk. As its bark ages the depth of valleys cause us to look and almost see and taste the history this tree has witnessed. How often have you leaned against a tree and wondered at the sights it has been allowed to have move across its bark?

We have energy surrounding... within   without .... always, and very much...borrowed, or could it be said, should it be whispered, the only thing not borrowed, is our soul...

::

::::::did I even sleep?

The gatekeeper time clock once again seems happy it has me captive. “Transaction accepted,” “I’ll show you accepted.” I grumble and head for the locker room to get my trauma scissors. Walking past bay twenty six I see one of my most familiar patients. She enjoys swallowing razor blades and putting glass up her rectum. Or anything she wishes to put up there. “Hello Marie, you are back to visit us?” She is not a tall woman, and the hospital gown barely fits over her stomach. But I can see that light inside her. She has demons messing with her mind twisting thoughts. Everyone is visited by these demons at one time or another. Some of them hide reality so one can continue to walk in the flesh. Maybe these are not bad demons. I haven’t quite figured that one out yet. But her demons stem from abuse during her youth. That and the chemical nature of humans, delicate is the balance with the brain.

Marks of self mutilation cover her arms and her neck. Her brown hair just touches her shoulders but she smiles when she sees me. She knows I don't judge her at all, she also sees into the others. It is far down inside her soul but the light of life is still finding moments in the sun. That sun is being able to just walk with the normal pod people on earth. I always see the normal ones of blank stare pod people. Their minds have gone into complacency mode, lost in nothing, searching for nothing, just circling in the air waiting to drop into non existence.

Psych will no longer see her, because she is non compliant. Against the law, yes, but who is going to listen to a self mutilator and someone that enjoys swallowing and shoving glass and assorted very sharp objects into their body cavities. Her bay is empty, nothing but the stretcher is in the room. All of the counter equipment and the suction canisters are removed. She is known to put anything up her so it is a precaution. The docs won't do anything to help her, they talk 'at' her and whisk her to the OR or to psych. Whichever seems the most needed at the moment. I have an affinity for this soul. Maybe she is a test for others to check their humanity and not check it at the door. Maybe she just chose this path long before birth. Or, just the consequences of horrendous abuse left her mind shattered. Whatever the cause, I treat her with respect.

“Hi Jared,” she smiles brightly when she sees me. Leaning against the door of the room, she holds the back of her gown together and looks to the floor. “We have to stop meeting like this Marie.” Smiling, I touch her shoulder and ask in a whisper, “are you ok today?” “Yea, just wanted to swallow a razor or two.” She smiles again and giggles. “I am about to go off in a little bit you better leave.” I walk into the room, “sit down on the stretcher with me for a bit Marie lets talk.” She moves slowly still holding her gown closed so as not to show her naked back. She is on a hold, so her clothes are locked away.

I can see the halls of dark in her mixing with twisted corners of light. I also see the cry for help from a small girl deep inside her core. The small girl that was alive at one time before abuse. Now gone inside the core of this tortured mind. One of the docs comes in to talk with her, I stay and wait for him to leave. "What did you do this for Marie and why do you keep doing it?” She looks at me and smiles. I feel the energy shift within her. Standing quickly I get in front of the doc just before she swings to hit him. I catch her fist, but the spew of vulgarity now has found its mark.

The doc is being cursed at in a language unknown to man. It is a language of the demons, I assume. I hold her arm, then lean to make eye contact with her. “Marie...come back out and play.” She immediately relaxes in my hold. Her smile of slow begins once more. The doc is gone, gone just as she raised her fist. “So do you feel better now?” She sits on the stretcher lowering her head. But her smile has not left. “You are a good person Jared, but you better leave I’m going to go off again.” I walk out of the room but look into her eyes before I do. “I see you in there Marie, don’t give up ok?” She giggles again, then her face changes to a frown.

She sits then lies on the stretcher. Quiet and wanting to sleep. I leave her there feeling the presence of the many forces enjoying the play in her mind. I am not able or allowed to help her away from the demons she has chosen to live within her. She has the path now, it is in the hands of all around her to allow her light to be seen.

My walk to the locker is now filling with those thoughts of wanting away from this ER. Too much darkness, too many falling into a place I wish to not be around anymore. The ocean is where I wish to be. The ocean, walking the beach finding agates and panning for gold. Contrary to popular belief one can pan for gold on the coast of Oregon. Smiling at the thought of this. My step is lighter. My locker awaits the deposit of the outside things, wallet, keys, phone, and the withdraw of the ER things. Scissors to cut clothes off of patients. Some already dead. Some paralyzed, some just wanting to die. With that flash that can find a mind, I see the many patients I have used this pair of scissors on.

Dead with blood still oozing, paralyzed with silent tears from the face of the body now unable to move. She was young, he was old, they were someone's love, and they are dead. Tossing the flash back into my ever filling pan of memories I straighten myself to stand as tall as I can to begin one more day. "Enough of this drama," I smack my head to remove the thoughts of redundant negative. Everything happens for a reason, so get your ass to work.

:::

I was zapped with tickling

wiggling from time

as I played with the faery

now a friend of mine

::::

I am back to the land of OZ. Another nickname I have given the ER.

Time does something that I know of, but am not happy with. It shifts and slows. Now the feel of all spiritual is clear to me. I feel the entities talking to patients pushing their vulgarity into their ears, into their souls as I walk through the ER looking for the night tech to get report on my new day of interactions and duties of bedpans and blood draws. Shaking my head I want away from this visual. Suddenly one walks up to me, invisible but visible in a not comfy way. Stepping through the energy I push my step past the non that wants to distract me and drain me. The dark ones have an agenda. I am not in the mood. I also feel it turn as if to look at me. Following my walk with its glance, I do not turn around to give it satisfaction. Yes, this is sounding crazy, it is a slight feel and I feel it. Cannot explain it but it happens and it is there. Energy we all are, energy never dies, energy just is.

I have to arrange the levels of concentration within my core to control this gift and the negatives of life. Energy flows, gotta have the right current to handle it. Good and evil, just different levels of life. Demons are real, angels are real, so pick which one you want to party with.

Stopping at the phlebotomist desk I notice the bay across has a patient struggling to lie down. Blood falls away from this person. A pool of blood is beside the stretcher. His clothes are covered with blood and torn. The patient is lying in a pool of blood. There is that blood again. Turning away from this I walk to the next patient. She lies there. I have blood order to pull from her blood that will tell what? I see no reason behind this futile moment. She is dead but alive. A Jane Doe. Her wallet contains a will stating where and to whom to give her things to. She was prepared to die..

Either you are very nosey or something very horrible has happened to me. She continues throughout the piece of paper that had been folded in her wallet. She told of who would get her property down to the last penny in her accounts. I look at her lying lifeless on the stretcher with the vent breathing for her. Her hair golden her nails freshly painted with a red that shines. "We hang on to life so hard or is it the body just doesn't want to let go of its fleshly life?" My thoughts again are finding voice. Walking past the next patient I am looking at each one this day. I am trying to find a reason to continue working in this place of blood with spit thrown at your face in an instant.

Death walking with life, entities near waiting as if the ER and the hospital are a virtual portal for the after life. As soon as that thought flicks its way into me I see a patient whose eyes have a shine within that almost knock me over. He will die, he has just been diagnosed with lung cancer. His family is calm.

I reach to help the man to a more comfortable place on the stretcher. "Need anything?" The wife smiles at me, the children are grown. "No thank you sweetie." She answers softly. Her eyes are red from crying, her hand is on his. The man has a strength unlike anything I have ever felt. I send a wish of light across this mans soul. The man looks over at me the very instant I had the wish,. catching me off guard some. "Thank you." The man says calmly as he pulls his wife's hand closer. I step back and away. The grown children look like the man of soon death. They reach with silent eyes wanting him ok, needing him ok, but allowing the moment they are in with him, as they stand there, to be special.

The docs are in a room with a patient. The patient, has somehow swallowed his retainer The X-ray is held up for the guy to see his partial half way down his throat. The ENT's are excited, Tthis is one for the books." They say to him excited and happy to have something new to do to a patient. The man is having trouble breathing. Contrasts, a team of happy young docs and a scared man hoping he can breathe. The young docs are ready to get him to the OR. He is ready to feel normal again.

I am in a fog of the worlds of two times. Two places, but they exist in one time and one place. Knowing the reality of reality is non, finding it daily with every walk my steps show the lack of life in life. We are in a place of tests and growth of levels. The man with lung cancer is in a place of entities and final destinations.

When the grim reaper finds, your hand is it going to be clean so you can go play with the fun boys? Or is it dirty with ugly of choices in life? Shaking my head at the thought of the waste of so many peoples lives caught up in material things. Is having money and a home and a shiny car worth taking your forever away? Forever in a place of dark and cold and scary just to claim the physical of a moment, a slight moment of pleasure here on this place of non reality. "Yea they like their stuff enough to kill you for it."

~~~~~~

I leave the ER to walk outside and away for a moment.
~~~~~~

I am trying to let go of this new pain. Tears now own my face, releasing is an interesting feel. The pour of water from depth of pain, that kind of pain everyone knows and most hold onto. I bury my head in my hands. Weeping my sobs are heard inside the ER, I am standing just outside the ambulance bay doors. I walk away from the hospital, toward my car. The ocean is where I want to be and right now. My insides are shattering with fragments of past knowledge of past ways of thought falling away then dropping like razors against my skin. I have to turn around, I can't leave, why can't I leave? I am done with this place of energy, of death, of puke of sorry of brains on the floor. Flashing my mind sweeps me once more with the jagged atrocities I have seen that people have created, caused fall into and live.

Wiping my tears away I push my ID against the door waiting for the beep that will allow me back inside the crapper. "Yea the crapper that's what I will call this hospital."

As soon as I enter one of the docs calls me in to help roll a patient off of a backboard. I hesitate, but follow the doc inside the room. The man is restrained to the board naked and full of stun gun torpedo's. Security follows me into the room. They will release him from the restraints, while the doc removes him from the board then will secure the patient to the bed. I see leaves all over this naked mans body.

The man is angry but obviously drunk or on something. “Where are my clothes?” He screams. If words were spit it would have caught me right in the eyes. The wave of anger and energy catch me off guard. I yell back at the patient. “You came in here without any!” Everyone stills in the room well everyone but the patient. He just continues to be repetitive and redundant. The doc smiles at me, not used to seeing me lose control. “He left his house naked today to attack the garbage man.” I laugh hard but the man keeps yelling for his clothes. “Why did you attack the garbage man? What did you think he was a monster?” I was messing with this patient something that is usually not my way. The other garbage guy called the police. They had to tase him to get to him. So here he is in my ER naked as a jaybird pleading innocence blaming all in the room on his moment of restraints and nakedness. I throw a sheet over him and walk out.

:::

..sippin on a soda..

walking with the sun..

seeing flowers grow

..now my day is done :)

“”””

I am pulled once more into a room to help with a patient. This time a female patient that the nurse needs help putting a catheter in. “Great,” is all that escapes my mouth. The lady is very large so I have to pull one thigh away for the nurse to push the catheter into its proper place.. The nurse struggles to find the proper hole. I pull the large leg open more. The catheter begins to be inserted and the lady screams grabbing my arm. As soon as she touches me she begins to moan. Looking at the nurse wondering what the hell is she moaning about. The nurse is pushing and pushing but nothing is going in. The patient now starts to stroke my arm as she moans more. The nurse begins to laugh trying to subdue the sounds so the lady doesn’t hear her. I lean to whisper. “You need to go lower for god sakes she is enjoying this.” The lady begins to squeeze my arm now while pushing her leg against my stomach.

She arches some, wanting more of the catheter to touch her. The nurse finally puts it in the right place. The moaning is replaced with a yell of pain. She lets go of my arm quickly tries to close her legs to this new feel. The nurse finishes putting the catheter into her bladder. I let go of the ladies leg. But she suddenly grabs my arm again, “what do you need?" “I need you, I am single and looking are you interested?” The nurse laughs now with a comment, “yes Jared is single do you want me to give you a phone number?”

"Sorry I am not single but your offer is very generous." I walk out of the room pulling my gloves off and snapping them at the nurse. "Look ashamed!" I smile and walk toward the back of the ER "Sheesh this place is crazy." Two steps further and I am pulled into yet another room. "Jared quick, we need you!" The patient's heart has stopped beating. I begin compressions. With each push I can feel the ladies soul leave the body. Slowly but surely it is squeezing out of the flesh. The nurses rush in with meds. I see the energy lingering now. Sweat forms on my forehead. Pushing harder I feel it is not this ladies time to leave. She slowly falls back into her body. In that instant she coughs. "Stop compressions." The nurse feels for a pulse. "She has a pulse." I step away from the lady and out of the room. Worn out from pushing but happy it has a good ending. For the moment anyway.

Vomit flies in front of me. The good ole projectile kind. The patient is holding onto the rail of the stretcher is vomiting everywhere. Stepping around the puke I am called yet once more to do a job. Kat calls for me to do an EKG quickly on the lady that I just did compressions on. Kat knows her stuff but can bother the hell out of a tech. In the middle of chaos she will want you to clean a patients mouth or prop a leg.

Always the patient's care but sometimes requesting some labor intensive duties during hectic moments.. The EKG machine is now in front of me and away I go. The tags go on the body to get the tracing for the EKG. Her skin is wet from sweat and bones are brittle. I can see her broken ribs from me pushing on her chest, doing compressions does help the heart push blood through the body but it also breaks ribs in the process. Finishing the EKG quickly I hand it to the doc.

There is a page overhead for another EKG and to transport one of my patients to ultrasound. As soon as they hand me the EKG slip for the next patient, another doc comes up wanting the blood results from an earlier enzyme test. One of the nurses yells at me "go get that patient in ultrasound Jared!" "I need the results of the enzymes Jared where are they?" "We need this EKG now..Jared!"

Now I know what it's like to be in a tornado. Pushing the EKG machine to the side I have to walk away and step outside or I will lose myself in this tornado. A tech does all, wipes the butts, dumps the urine, collects the blood, does the EKG's that are ordered, bags the deads. All the patient care that makes the hospital look good, and for what pay? Nada, patada. I am done.

The hospital, every hospital is a virtual revolving door for the other side of life. With the constant passing of lives the door swings always open, thus the fine line of reality and spirituality, filling with demons and angels. They travel easily through the building looking for those souls that are about to find out why they should have been a little bit nicer while they were alive.

Or, those to be thankful they gave a lean of help and gentle into other peoples day. Suffer the reward if you fling your spit into the hearts of life. It will not be a pleasant journey for you for a long time.

These energies enjoy invading the rooms with a heavy feel of fear or sadness. Inundating the innocent visitors with that feel of doom and fear but there is also the ones of pure love. They find and surround the ones who chose in life to give and show compassion.

Once in the burn unit, the feel was of very very bad. One of the trauma nurses told me of a black entity that left from a freshly dead patient. This black entity moved quickly past the nurse station, then slamming open two magnetically locked doors. She said of how the doors bowed first, then the magnets gave. She also said I was the only one that she could tell, for she was alone on the floor at the time and she didn't want to be sent to the psych floor. People of pod head strength have no clue about energies that do exist, the crazy label has been slapped on many that were truly just given a gift of sight. A gift? A curse? A wish, a nurse? rhyming is so much fun...

::::::

when time is still

and thoughts come clearly..

I know of forever..

and it is silly...

.....

My beach, my rocks, good energy and music cause my walk to turn toward the doors. The ambulance bay doors. Opening and closing like the mouth of a beast allowing it's prey to come inside. I am done, I feel great as I walk out of the door. My badge tossed to the floor. I quit. I hear faint voices calling for me but ignoring people at times is a blessing? The ambulances are parked neatly with their butts to the doors that never stop opening. I hear music, I hear... The song... I ignore it. Just a coincidence. The song that always seems to play then something bad happens. I hear it again from a car passing on the street as I head to the parking lot. It is louder and echoing. From the ambulances and from every car that now passes me, I hear the song of warning me. I ignore it..

Looking down at my black boots walking across the pavement, I am cool, nothing is needed to worry about, just keep walking. Looking up at the guard shack just outside the front of the employee parking lot I hear his radio playing. No and no and no. Everything is ok but my gut says, what the hell?

There it is, as I turn I see an elderly lady begin to cross the street. She is moving so slowly, her head is down. She is close to me. Looking around quickly I see the speeding car heading right for her. I can yell, she won't hear. I.. can yell..... The song in the guard shack is louder and resonating in my heart, my soul. Running now to her, I push her away to the sidewalk. The car.. hits me.

::::::Inside the walls of me..::

Time flashes somehow and I see my mother standing near a tunnel The light is grayish and I feel no pain. I feel comfy and yummy and happy and yummy, seeing my mother. Maybe She tried to warn me, she is showing me this now but I am slow sometimes. Words, I cannot describe the peace and joy, the safe feeling of here. Where is here? I see people run to me while I'm lying on the street. Blood is coming from my head, my ears. "Oh, that's not good" I feel myself think this thought. Someone walks up and throws a coat over me. "This person is dead". "I am not dead!" I say in a place where words exist in a different way. "That coat has to come off of me, not liking this at all." I can feel my heart pounding very fast. It is pounding hard, I hear it I feel it, I don't like it.

Suddenly a flash again, I am in the trauma room, I recognize all the people the docs, I see myself while the nurses wipe blood from my head. I just want them to stop rubbing the blood off of my face.

Awakened by a catheter, what a blessing, who knew? I feel them put it into my bladder. Looking around I see the familiar faces. Instead of watching them work on me from the other side of reality, I am back to the land of the living. Great, I try to leave and end up on my back as a patient.

Falling away into a wonderfully drugged state I relax into nowhere land. I am broken, right femur, clavicle, open ankle fracture, the worst I might add.

Time does its thing and I am released, on crutches with pain meds and well wishers. I will return to work at the ER when I am well enough. I watch my black boots move across the pavement as I crutch my way to my youngest daughter's car. The pain pills are kicking in and I am liking the way I feel. Soon to return to the battlefield of sick and death but I will be more prepared now that I have been on the receiving end of pain.

The End

Wait.. there isn't a body bag being zipped up over my face and my breath still moves ... so it's not the end……

::

Calm with slow

know your every moment ..is put carefully down

a report card.. for... when you slip across that place of time and .. die………

About the author:::

Worked the ER as a tech was an EMT is the parent of three daughters and two grandsons. Loves the Oregon coast and the rocks that roll up on the beach. Cycling, doing weights, traveling, staying at hotels, wrapping rocks, and writing…

Time of Death The Story of Jared: A graphic journey of an ER tech is the book written from this journal. If you wish a story line with romance and spiritual get yourself a copy.

On The Edge of Evil, a romantic suspense, you will not guess the ending.

When you pass to that side of forever::: tell my Mom and Dad ::hello. God bless all.. carry love in your hearts.

Made in United States
North Haven, CT
09 November 2021